THE
MISSING PIECE

MIRA JEFFREYS

BWP
BETTER WORLD PRESS
GARDNER, KANSAS 66030

Copyright © 2020 Mira Jeffreys
Print Edition: ISBN 978-1-7923-4297-4
Library of Congress Control Number: 2020919434

All rights reserved. This book or any portion thereof
may not be reproduced or used in any manner whatsoever without the express written permission of the publisher except for the use of brief quotations in a book review.

The Missing Piece is a work of fiction. Names, characters, locations, business, events and incidents are the products of the author's imagination. Any resemblance to actual persons, living or dead, or actual events is purely coincidental.

Printed & Bound in the United States of America

First Printing, 2020
Cover Design by JennJ Designs jennjdesigns.com

Visit Mira Jeffreys online at:
WWW.MIRAJEFFREYS.COM

For Madison 🖤
THE PERFECT DAUGHTER

*E*mma's heart stopped for a millisecond; not very long, but long enough to steal her breath away. She cupped her mouth before she could scream. This couldn't be right. She glanced up at the mirror and the person staring back frightened her.

"What have I done?" The question came out as a mere whisper and was instantly drowned out by the sound of a toilet flushing in one of the stalls. She scrambled to clear the box and wrappers from the sink, swiping them quickly into the trash bin. Sliding the test wand into the front pocket of her apron, she quickly turned on the faucet and splashed her face with cool water.

She knew she needed to calm down. She felt faint and there was no way she could go back on the floor looking like this. She gazed at her reflection again. After a night of tossing and turning, she looked terrible. Today was supposed to be a normal day.

"Hey, Em." Lexie greeted her when she appeared at the sink next to her.

"Hey, Lex. How's it going?"

Lexie turned on the water and washed her hands for a solid thirty seconds before answering. Emma counted. It was an excruciatingly long thirty seconds, too. She knew what was coming. Lexie had been stocking the shelves on the health and beauty aisle when Emma came up and picked out a test.

Emma waited. And waited. She almost took the opportunity to escape, but she knew she couldn't do that to Lexie. She was her best friend. Lexie had always been there for her and even though she'd really like to be alone right now, she knew she needed her. She owed her an explanation. Finally, Lexie turned off the water and turned towards her.

"So, what's the answer?"

"Answer?" Emma knew better than to pretend with her, but she had to keep the front up. Lexie could always see through Emma's façade.

"Don't insult my intelligence, Em. I saw you pick it up and then you took an unscheduled lunch break, so are you going to tell me what's going on?"

Emma sighed and leaned against the wall. She took the test wand out of her apron pocket and handed it to Lexie.

Lexie couldn't hide the shock on her face. "Oh crap."

"That's what I said."

"Is it Cal's?"

THE MISSING PIECE

Emma splashed some more water on her face before answering. She knew whose it was but saying it out loud just made it worse. "Yes," Emma said. She hung her head over the sink, doing her best to keep her tears inside. Just when she thought she had recovered from the last thing she did that shamed her parents, Now this. She should have known better. She did know better. She just wasn't thinking straight.

"That's great! I mean, that's good isn't it?"

"I'm still trying to wrap my mind around this."

"Are you going to tell him?"

"No."

"Why not?"

Emma spun around to face her. "Because I don't want to tell him right now! I mean, this is a nightmare."

"How is it a nightmare? You guys are dating. You love him."

"Yeah, I do, but I'm not too sure if he loves me like I love him. If I tell him this, he'll leave. And not only that, my parents are going to flip when they find this out."

Lexie put her arm around her. "Em, not all guys are bad. Cal is a really nice guy and he cares about you. You know that."

"This will change everything."

"For the better."

"You're such an optimist."

"It's good to be an optimist. In this case, I must be the one to say that Cal has a right to know."

"Yeah, I know."

"He's a good guy. He's got a supportive family, a secure job, his own place... Need I go on?"

"I get all of that, but I'm just not sure that he and I are on the same page. He thinks I should take more advantage of the things my parents have and follow in their footsteps, but I don't want to do that. Sometimes I think he's only with me because of who my family is."

The bathroom door swung open and in came one of their coworkers. She ignored them as she made her way to the back of the bathroom and into one of the vacant stalls. Lexie pulled her friend closer.

"You are a beautiful person, Em. Inside and out. This is just your insecurity talking. Cal isn't with you just because you're a Benson. He's with you because you're Emma."

"Yeah, I guess."

"Why are you so down on yourself? This doesn't sound like you."

Emma lowered her head again.

"Talk to me, Em."

"I just have a lot going on right now. This adds to my stress."

"What's going on?"

"Do you remember when I paid the private detective to find my birth mother?"

"Yeah?"

"Well, he couldn't find her."

"He couldn't find out anything about her?"

"I mean, he just found a name but nothing more than that. I paid three grand for a name! I was really hoping that he could find her and talk to her, you know."

"A name is better than nothing, Em."

"Yeah, I know. I just wish I knew where I belong."

"You belong here. This is your home."

"You know what I mean."

"I'm sorry this's gotten you down."

"And now with this news here," she said, swinging the wand around in the air, "I need to know."

"Listen, I can't even pretend to understand what you're going through right now, but what other options do you have?"

"You're the optimistic one. Why don't you tell me?"

"Have you ever thought about looking for her yourself?"

"Yeah, when I was a kid."

"Maybe that's what you need to do. Do it yourself."

"That sounds great and all, but I wouldn't even know where to start!"

The toilet flushed in the back and the coworker came to the sink. She washed her hands and left without saying a word to them.

"Can we finish talking about this tonight?" Lexie asked.

"Tonight?"

"Yeah, I'm coming over and we're going to have some pizza and talk about this."

"I don't feel like company."

"Well, maybe not now, but how do you know you won't feel like company later?"

Sometimes, she wished Lexie wouldn't be so persistent. She just wanted to go home after work and wallow in her misery. "Fine," she agreed.

"Great. I'll pick up the pizza on the way."

"What time?"

"Seven-thirty. That gives me enough time to get home and finish writing my paper."

"You're not done with that paper yet?"

"Almost. You know I'm a perfectionist."

They shared a laugh. "You're going to be a great counselor. You care so much about people," Emma said.

"Caring comes easy for me, but it's gotten me burned a lot."

"But it hasn't seemed to discourage you at all. I wish I were more like you."

"And I wish I were more like you. I need to get back on those aisles before Jerkwad Jimmy comes looking for me."

Emma laughed and pushed her out the door. "Go! Don't get yourself in trouble over me."

"See you tonight!"

After closing the door, Emma walked back over to the sink and gazed at herself once more in the mirror. Sweat beaded her forehead and she felt lightheaded.

She took a deep breath and splashed her face one last time. "Time to put your game face on, Em." She smiled at her reflection and disappeared out the door.

*E*mma bolted off the couch when the doorbell rang. She squinted at the clock. It was seven forty-five. "Man, hold your horses!"

"Hurry up and open the door," Lexie called from the other side. "The pizza's getting cold."

Emma swung open the door and motioned for her to come in, "Sorry, I dozed off."

"I've been standing out there for ten minutes waiting for you to answer."

"I said I was sorry."

"Anyways, let's eat." She plopped the pizza down on the coffee table and opened the box. "Our favorite. Double pepperoni, mushrooms, olives, and extra cheese."

Emma's stomach turned. She hadn't eaten all day and should be famished by now, but the thought of eating pizza didn't settle well with her. Especially not when she noticed the grease dripping from the slice that Lexie had picked up.

As she watched Lexie sink her teeth into it, her stomach twisted and tightened. "I'll be right back," she gasped as she ran to the to the bathroom and shut the door behind her.

Ten minutes later she resurfaced and found Lexie pigging out on her third slice of pizza and browsing through Netflix. Lexie looked up and shrugged.

"I know I should've helped you, but you know I hate puke."

"I understand." Emma walked over to the fridge and pulled out a couple of water bottles. "I hate it, too."

Lexie took the offered bottle and sighed. "Besides the puking, do you feel any different?"

Emma shrugged. "Just a little scared."

"Of what?"

"I don't know. Scared that I'm not going to know what to do, maybe."

"Are you going to keep it?"

"Yes."

"No one would blame you if you –"

"I'm keeping it."

"Okay. I'll support you either way, you know that."

"Yeah, I know, but I'm keeping it."

"All right," Lexie said quietly and placed her water on the table. "Let's talk about what's bothering you."

"That would take all night. Don't you work tomorrow?"

"Nope and neither do you. I checked the schedule before I left."

Emma leaned back on the couch. "I'm afraid to tell my parents."

"No kidding. They're going to lose their minds! Especially your mom."

"Don't remind me. She already thinks I'm a failure."

"Aww, I'm sure that's not true."

"It is. She said so."

"Really?"

"Yep. Not too long after I quit my classes in freshman year. She said she should've known better than to pick a child like me and she wished she could go back and pick a different one."

"Oh my God, that's terrible! What did she mean, a child like you?"

"God as my witness, she said it."

"How does your dad feel? I mean, is he supportive?"

"Well, kinda. Dad is just Dad. He doesn't get involved much. He's always just been there. Mom runs the house."

"That's crazy."

"She's critical of everyone and everything I get involved with."

"I'm sorry, Em."

"I haven't told her that you and I are as close as we are because I know as soon as I do, she'll start chipping away at your character like she does everyone else's."

"I hate how controlling she is. I know it would be hard, but maybe you should just cut ties with them. Especially since she wished she had adopted another kid!"

"Yeah." She sighed heavily. "They'll probably take care of that once they find out. I think they're looking for an excuse to cut me off for good."

"Are you serious?"

"Yeah. I went to check on my college savings account and it was all gone. I found out later from the bank that my mom withdrew all the money and closed the account. Just because I dropped out, doesn't mean that money didn't belong to me. It could have gone toward pursuing a career. But since I didn't do it her way, I lost out."

"I can't believe they did that. That's ultimate control, you know that, right?"

Emma nodded. She tried not to think about the fact that her parents controlled her, but it was the reality of her life. She made one stupid mistake and they deemed her unfit to handle her own money.

"They can keep it for all I care. I'm working and I'm saving. I just wish I hadn't dented my bank account by paying the private investigator."

"I admire you for taking a stand like you did. I mean, you're Emma Benson and you're working at our store."

Emma laughed. "Really, Lex?"

"Yes, really. Everybody knows you don't really have to work there. You just do."

"It's not really noble. I'm just doing it to piss off my parents."

They laughed together. "I'm going to wait awhile before breaking the news to them. If I decide to tell them, I want to do it only after I've told Cal. Then if he leaves, I'll still have them, you know."

"And you'll still have me," Lexie said.

"Yes, I'll still have you. You know what I meant."

Lexie laughed and picked a piece of pepperoni off the pizza. "So how do you think Cal will react?"

Emma took a few seconds to look down at her hands folded in her lap. "Honestly, I think he'll be shocked, but I hope he'll be happy."

"You said earlier that you don't think he's on the same page as you. What makes you say that?"

"Like you said, I'm probably just being insecure." Emma searched her friend's eyes to see if she agreed.

"Has he mentioned marriage?"

"Yeah, very briefly. We were watching some romcom and he made a comment about how he thought I'd be a high-maintenance wife."

Lexie chuckled. "He's right about that."

"You're not funny. I'm very easy to please."

Lexie nudged her with her shoulder. "Just joking, Em. Lighten up."

Emma wished she could lighten up. Everything was crashing in on her so fast that she couldn't see the light at the end of the tunnel. "I should've been more careful," she said.

"But you've made the decision to keep it, right?"

"Yeah."

"Then all you can do is accept it and move on."

Emma glanced up at the ceiling. If only it was that easy. "I'm trying, Lex. I'm just really stressed out."

"About the baby?"

"Yes, mostly. And I'm scared."

"Of what?"

Emma kept silent for a few minutes and Lexie didn't rush her for an answer. Eventually she glanced over at Lexie. "I wish I knew."

"You've got to know what you're afraid of."

"Usually I could answer that question, but right now I'm having a hard time working through my feelings."

Lexie listened quietly.

"I can't believe I have a life growing inside of me. I could never think of giving it up like my birth mother did me. I'm not selfish like she was."

"Maybe she had a good reason, Em."

"Good reason?" she laughed. "Is there ever a good reason to give up a child for adoption?"

"Well actually, yes, there are plenty of good reasons women choose to give up their children. Maybe one of those reasons happened to her."

Emma squeezed her eyes tightly shut. She'd done her research, she knows of at least ten different reasons why women gave up their child, but none of those reasons mattered. The fact remains that her birth mother didn't want her.

"Em," Lexie said softly, "How long are you going to hold on to this?"

"As long as it takes. Maybe I'll stop feeling the way I do if and when I find her."

"I'm so mad at your mom for the way she did this. She could've waited."

Memories of the night she was told that she was adopted flooded back into her mind. Her parents waited until she'd blown out her ten candles and then they revealed that she was adopted. It never ceased to amaze her how quickly the illusion of her life was shattered. The ugly truth: She was a just some charity kid that her parents felt sorry for.

"It was better that way. At least I didn't have to believe the lie very long."

"I wish I had a solution to make you feel better."

"It's okay. It's just one of those things that I need to go through. Right now, knowing that I'm gonna have a baby makes me more determined to find my birth mother and get some answers."

"Will finding her give you closure?"

"Maybe."

"Then I hope with all my heart that you find her."

"Me too, Lex. And if I do, then I can start living."

"Aww, Em," Lexie said as she hugged her tightly. "You're going to be a good mom."

"I don't know about that. My mom didn't hug me and cuddle me or do any of those things mothers are supposed to do. I don't know how."

"You'll do just fine. It comes naturally I heard," Lexie said.

"I guess then that's why my mom was so cold with me." Emma leaned back against the couch and stared at the ceiling again. "Because I wasn't her own, so it wasn't natural."

"I'm sorry that your mom didn't love you like you deserved, but just because she didn't do it for you doesn't mean that you're going to do the same to yours," Lexie said.

"How can you be so sure?"

"Because I know you and underneath that hard Benson layer is the kindest, most warm-hearted person I've ever met."

"Oh, Lex! That's the sweetest thing you've ever said to me."

"It's the truth. I know the real you and you're not like them. Stop being so hard on yourself. Whoever your birth mother is, I have a feeling that you're just like her."

Emma hugged Lexie again, this time holding on tighter than before. She wanted to release the tears she'd been holding in, but couldn't. There was a time and place for everything, and now wasn't the time to break down.

Her phone started ringing. She picked it up off the coffee table and checked the caller ID. It was Cal. She let it ring. He'd hear the emotion in her voice and press her for answers. All she wanted was a little peace right now.

"I'll call him back later."

"Stop stressing about telling him. Everything is going to work out. He's going to be happy, Em. And I'm willing to bet he'll ask you to marry him."

"You think so?"

"Absolutely. I mean look at his family. Traditional Irish Americans. They're all about family! Have you forgotten that you eat dinner with them every Sunday? How much more serious could this relationship get?"

"I hadn't thought about it like that."

"Well you should. He's probably already bought you a ring. This news will set everything in motion."

"You're so optimistic."

"Relax, Em. We're going to be planning a wedding soon."

Emma laughed and played with her ring finger. It'd be nice to reach down one day and feel a ring there. She loved Cal more than anyone who came before him.

"Thanks, Lex. I'm feeling better about all of this. You're such a great friend."

"I'm the real deal, Em. I'm always going to be here for you."

Emma smiled, comforted by that fact.

"So, if you find your birth mother, what questions are you going to ask her?"

Emma shrugged. "I just want to know why."

"Why what?"

"Why she didn't want me."

"Aww, Em."

"I've gone my entire life feeling like I've done something wrong and that was why my mom didn't hug me or tell me she loved me." Emma sighed and leaned against the arm of the couch. "I just wish I knew who I was."

A period of silence followed as her statement hung in the air above them.

"Why don't you go find out?" Lexie said.

Emma frowned at her. "How?"

"The same way the private investigator did, just do a better job than him."

"What are you getting at?"

"I say you follow up on whatever lead you have and go find out for yourself who you are."

"Are you serious?"

"Yes. What do you have to lose?"

"My job."

"You hate it anyway. Plus, your folks are super rich, Em. They're snobby, yeah, but they're not going to turn their backs on you. That's too much negative publicity."

"Yeah, I guess you're right."

"Maybe this is the universe telling you that it's time to find your mother."

"I don't know about that, Lex."

"All I'm saying is that if you feel this incredible desire to know who you are, then maybe it's time you found out."

Emma thought it over. Lexie was probably right. Even when she tried to put the thoughts of finding her birth mother out of her mind, she couldn't do it. It was everything she thought about these days.

"I would have to put in for a leave of absence. Do you think management will accept it?"

"Can't hurt to try."

"I like the idea, but I'm nervous about this. I told you what happened the last time I took a trip across the country. What if something goes wrong?"

"What could go wrong?"

"I don't know. What if I get a flat?"

Lexie rolled her eyes. "Then you change it."

"What if I get lost?"

"That's what Siri is for."

"What if the money runs out? I couldn't call my parents and ask them to transfer money especially if they find out I'm looking for my mother."

"Then you just call me, and I'll put it into your account." Lexie nodded once as though it was settled.

"Dang it, Lex!"

Lexie laughed and patted Emma on the leg. "For every one of your excuses, I'll have a solution. So, quit trying."

Emma took a deep breath. She had two choices. She could either forget about the search or she could go find the answers she needed.

"What if I find her and she doesn't want anything to do with me?"

"Then at least you tried."

"All right. I think I'm going to try to find her myself."

"That's great. Do you need some money?"

"I don't think so. I should be okay if I play my cards right."

"But just in case, let's make sure you have extra cash."

"Okay. Good idea." Emma said.

"What are you going to do about Cal?"

Emma chewed on her bottom lip. "I'll tell him everything on Sunday after dinner."

"Good. I'm so proud of you, Em."

"Why is this so important to you?"

"Because I want to see you happy. You deserve to be happy."

"And you think Cal will make me happy?"

"You smile a lot more when he's around. I just wish you'd stop fighting it so much."

Emma nodded. "Maybe you're right. Thanks, Lex."

"You're welcome."

"I think I'm going to go to bed now. I'm exhausted."

"Okay. Do you mind if I hang out here for a little bit?"

"Sure, as long as you don't bother me in the middle of the night. You know where everything is."

"Awesome, thanks!"

"Oh, and please don't turn the tv up too loud. I've had trouble sleeping lately."

Lexie gave her a quick salute and flipped on the tv. Emma laughed to herself and went off to bed.

For the first time in seven months, Emma arrived late for dinner. She'd lost track of time rehearsing how she was going to tell him. Every time, she came up with some new way to say it, it just ended up sounding practiced and robotic. All she could hope for was to come up with something at the last minute, something that didn't sound so... unemotional.

After dinner, Cal walked Emma down to the lake on his parents' property. She loved it there. It was so peaceful, and she always enjoyed sitting by it, watching the ducks swim by.

She imagined how carefree their lives must be. Just eating, sleeping, and swimming. If only she could switch places with them for a day.

"Emma?"

His voice tugged her out of her thoughts. She loved his voice. It was strong but gentle, and his light Irish accent was one of the many things that had attracted her to him in the first place.

"Sorry, my mind was someplace else."

"I noticed," he said, scooting closer to her. "I'm going to be honest, I'm nervous about this talk of ours."

She nodded. She took a deep and cleansing breath. "You have been so good to me, Cal, and I want you to know that."

His brow furrowed into a deep frown. She could see him processing the sentence, dissecting it word for word while he waited for her to continue.

"I have some news for you and I'm not too sure how I'm going to tell you because I'm really nervous."

He straightened up and let go of her hand. "Just give it to me straight. There's no need to drag it out." He glanced out across the lake and sighed heavily. His square jaw tightened as he folded his arms across his chest.

Emma felt lightheaded. "Cal, I missed my period."

He turned and looked at her, but he didn't say anything for a while. "Did you take a test yet?"

"Yes," she said quietly. Her hands trembled. Everything about his body language made her realize that she'd misjudged how he might handle the news.

"And what's the verdict?"

"Verdict?"

"Yeah. Don't draw this out any longer than you have to. Just tell me if you're pregnant or not."

Her mouth dropped. His tone had cooled, sending chills running up her spine.

"Yes. I am."

He sighed and gazed out across the lake. "Wonderful." The sarcasm dripping from his lips preceded a laugh. "You gotta be kidding me."

"No. I'm not kidding. The test was positive."

"Who've you told about this?"

"No one but Lex, why?"

"Don't tell anyone else until we figure out what we're going to do about it."

"What we're going to do about it? I'm keeping it."

He glanced back at her. "Shouldn't that be both our decisions?"

"What do you mean?" As Emma stared into Cal's eyes, she came to the sad realization that she'd been wrong. Their relationship was fine as long as no extra variables were thrown into the mix.

"I'm not sure about this."

"I understand it's a surprise to you. This surprised me too, but I can't get rid of our baby. It doesn't even matter if we didn't plan it. It happened."

Cal got up and walked over to the edge of the lake. He picked up a rock and skipped it across. "A baby changes everything, Emma. You know that."

Her heart sunk. "I'm confused right now, Cal. I thought you'd be happy. I thought we were happy together."

He walked back over and sat down next to her. "Listen to me, okay?" He sighed and played with the watch on his arm. "I'm happy with you. We have a lot of fun together and I genuinely enjoy being with you, but I'm not ready to be a father."

"But—"

"I know you look at where I come from and assume, but that's the life my family wants for me. That's not what I want. I'll be happy if it stays just the two of us until I'm ready."

"Until you're ready?" She gasped.

"Yes."

"What about me? Do you think I wanted this to happen? It took both of us to make this baby."

"I know that."

"Then act like you know it!" She got up and nearly sprinted to the edge of the lake. She couldn't breathe. It felt like a cinderblock had been placed on her chest.

"Now's not the time to get angry," he said.

She spun around. "How can I not get angry? Here I am thinking that you'd be happy and want to do this with me, but then I realize that you're not. All you're thinking about is yourself."

"Would you calm down, please?"

"You don't care that this will change my life as well. You don't care that I'm going to have to adapt my entire life just to care for this baby."

"I do care, that's why I don't think you should go through with it."

"What?" She tried her best not to see him through different eyes, but what he said went against everything she thought she knew about him. It didn't make sense. These weren't his family values.

"Get rid of it while you can. We'll be more careful from here on out."

She couldn't bring herself to speak. The tears pooling in her eyes made it difficult to see his face. It was actually better this way. She didn't want to remember.

"I don't know what's gotten into you, Callum, but I'll never do such a thing!"

He shrugged and shook his head. "I don't want a kid right now."

"That's fine," she said, turning her back to him. She wiped the tears from her cheeks and turned back to face him. "I'll have to admit that I thought this was going to go way different than it did."

"Can you blame me? This is big, Emma. I'm not a father type of guy. Husband yeah, but not a father."

"Sure."

"Listen," he said, getting up from the bench. He walked over and put his arm around her. "Let's just go back inside and finish visiting with my family and then we can go back to my place and talk about this more?"

She shrugged out of his embrace and backed away from him. "There's nothing more to talk about. Obviously, we're on two different pages."

"We can still discuss it."

"What's there to discuss? I want to keep it and you don't. It's that simple."

"I can't get on board with this, Emma. Either you get rid of it or we need to take a break."

"Take a break?"

"Yeah."

"How dare you make me choose between this baby which you helped me make, and you. I don't understand."

"I'm not ready!"

"I'm not ready either! But there's no way I'm ending my pregnancy just to make you feel better."

His face hardened as he stepped away from her. "Suit yourself."

"What would your parents think if they knew you made this suggestion to me?"

He lowered his head.

"Yeah, that's what I thought." She laughed to keep herself from crying. "Don't worry. In case you've forgotten, I'm a Benson and I can take care of this baby without your help. I just thought you would like to know."

They stared at each other for what seemed like hours. Emma stared into the eyes of a man she used to know, but now she couldn't even recognize him. How could she have been so wrong? She knew he wouldn't do cartwheels, but she was so sure he'd be happy about the news.

Maybe she hadn't found the secret to happiness after all. And maybe happiness eluded her because she didn't really deserve it. All she knew was that she needed to make her exit so she could stay on schedule.

"Tell the O'Brannigans that dinner was great this week as always," she said, turning and walking up the gravel pathway towards the house.

He chased after her and caught her by the arm. "Why don't we go back inside and finish visiting?"

She yanked her arm from his grip. "I refuse to go back in there and pretend like you didn't just break up with me."

He sighed deeply. "I'm sorry. I just can't get on board with this right now. Just give me some time."

"You made that point very clear. And like I said, I can take care of this baby on my own. I just preferred it to be with you."

"I'm sorry but I can't."

"And that's your choice," she said, pushing him away. "And it's my choice to walk away before you hurt me any more than you already have."

"At least go back in there and say bye to my folks."

"If I go back in there, I'll tell them everything, including how you broke up with me because I won't get rid of our child."

When she realized he wasn't going to press the issue further, she ran back to her car and jumped in. She made sure she didn't breakdown while he was watching. She sped away down the street, her tears dangerously blurring her vision. Her entire life was crashing in slow motion and there wasn't anything she could do to stop it.

Emma jolted out of her sleep, rolled out of bed and wiped the sleep out of her eyes. She picked up her phone and squinted at the screen. "Seriously?" she groaned.

The door buzzed again.

She slipped into her nightshirt, made her way to the living room and peeked through the peephole. "What the heck is she doing here?" she gasped and opened the door. "Hey? What are you doing here so late?"

Ericka Benson resembled a mannequin in a window display. Always perfectly groomed, not even a hair was ever out of place. Her face had the same expression that Emma always saw when she looked at her. One of frustration and disapproval.

"Aren't you going to invite your mother in?" she asked.

"Oh. Um, sure. I'm sorry. You woke me," Emma said, stepping out of the way.

Ericka entered into the apartment, her judgmental eyes scanning everything in a matter of seconds. Had Emma known that she would get a surprise visit from her, she would have cleaned up before bed.

"Is something wrong? Why are you here so late?"

"I finished the fundraiser for the new city park, and I just thought I'd pay you a visit."

"Oh." Emma buttoned the rest of her shirt up and walked into the kitchen. "How much were you able to raise?"

"Two million."

"Oh, that's wonderful. The people are going to love the new park. That extra money will help them get done sooner."

"I suppose," she said, glancing around the room. "It could've been more if the patrons weren't being stingy tonight."

Emma cleared her throat. "Would you like something warm to drink? Coffee? Tea?"

Ericka took a seat on the couch. "Tea is fine."

"All right." Emma filled the teapot with water and placed it on the stove. "Is Dad with you?"

"No. I came alone."

"Okay." Emma stayed in the kitchen until the beverages were done and then she brought her mother a cup. She sat down beside her. "Are you okay?"

"Yes, I am."

"So why are you here? You never visit me this late."

Ericka nodded. "Your father told me you asked to borrow a large sum of money."

"Oh, I see. I asked him not to tell you."

Ericka chuckled and sipped from her cup. "There are no secrets between your father and I, dear. What do you need the money for?"

"It's personal."

"I would like to know."

"You don't need to know."

"Actually, I do. Especially if you plan on pulling another trick like you did in San Francisco."

"Do you always have to bring up San Francisco? That was a very painful time for me, Mom. Why can't you just let it go?"

"I was just reminding you of why I question your money managing skills."

"I manage my money just fine. I have my job, this place, I pay my bills, I'm never late. What more do you want from me?"

"I want you to start taking the life you've been given seriously! Stop living like poor people when you're a Benson. It's downright embarrassing."

"I take my life seriously!"

"Really now?"

"Yes." Emma took a sip of her tea, hoping to calm her nerves a little. No matter how hard she tried, she could never please Ericka.

"Your father and I have invested a lot of time and money into your upbringing. You are supposed to work by our model so that we can pass the Foundation on to you, but what do you do? You work at a grocery store for heaven's sake! No one who's important in the sector will ever take you seriously. All of my work has been in vain."

"There's nothing wrong with the way I live. I support the Benson Foundation by being there at almost every fundraiser. I do my part to help plan and pull all that crap together. And not one of the fundraisers I've organized has ever failed. Why can't that be good enough for you?"

"Because you're wasting your life doing this nonsense. You need to give the Foundation first priority in your life. You need to move out of this dump and back to the mansion with your father and I so we can make sure you're doing everything you need to do for the company."

"Are you serious?" Emma gasped and slammed her cup down on the table. "Are you being serious right now?"

"Of course, I'm serious. If you don't give the Foundation top priority in your life, your future financial security is at risk."

"Are you really threatening me right now?"

"I'm just suggesting that for once, you start making the right decisions for yourself."

Emma couldn't believe she came over here at this hour just to criticize her about her life choices. "I appreciate the suggestion." Emma wished that Ericka would leave. She already felt sick to her stomach from talking with her. Ericka had a way of stirring up some of the worst emotions that Emma tried to keep hidden.

"What are your plans with the O'Brannigan boy?"

THE MISSING PIECE

Ericka's question scraped across her heart. "No immediate plans, why?"

"Well that's good because his family isn't known in the community. You need to align yourself with someone who has more influence. You'll get further that way."

"It doesn't matter if the O'Brannigans aren't known like us, they're good people. That's all that should matter to you and Dad."

"What matters is knowing you'll end up marrying a stable man who knows how to handle his money and someone who won't squander away your inheritance."

"I can make that decision for myself. It's up to me who I settle down with."

"True, but I hope you make a good decision that'll benefit you and whatever family you plan to have in the future."

Silence fell over them. Emma felt the burden of her mother's attitude weighing her down. "Why wasn't I ever good enough for you?"

"What?"

"Never mind," Emma said as she got up and went into the kitchen. "Would you like some more tea?"

"No, I'm fine."

After a couple of minutes, Emma rejoined her on the couch. "I get that you don't trust me yet with money, but it's been four years. I won't make a mistake like that again. I was young and in love. I was stupid."

Ericka sighed deeply.

"It's fine if you don't give it to me, but it would really help me get to where I'm going."

"Where are you going?"

"I'm sorry, but I can't tell you that."

Ericka nodded and patted Emma's hand, "Very well. If you can't tell me where you're going and why you need so much money, then I cannot help you."

Emma laughed and moved away from her. "All right. That's fine."

Ericka placed the teacup on the coffee table and stood up. "Please let your father and I know when you've made it back home safely." She leaned and kissed Emma on top of her head.

Emma held her tongue. There were so many words that wanted to come out, but none of them would do her any good at the moment.

"Goodbye, Mother."

"Goodnight, Em." Ericka let herself out of the apartment, slamming the door loudly behind her.

Emma went over to the window and peered down into the parking lot. A couple of minutes passed before she saw Ericka emerge from the building. The driver of the car got out and opened the door for her. Before ducking into the car, Ericka looked up.

Emma wished she knew why she didn't love her. She had to have done something wrong along the way to merit Ericka's scathing reproach. Whatever it was, Emma wasn't sure if their relationship could ever be fixed.

She waved goodbye and was surprised when Ericka waved back before disappearing into the car. As she watched the car drive away, she felt the sting of Ericka's rejection all over again.

4

Emma was packing the last of her things when Lexie walked in. She knew that, regardless of the time, Lexie would come when she called. It was nearing 3 a.m. and she was exhausted. After the talks with both Cal and Ericka, Emma needed a mental break.

Lexie appeared in her bedroom doorway holding a brown paper bag. "This better be good if you dragged me out of bed at two in the morning," she said as she took a seat on Emma's bed.

Emma took the bag from Lexie's hands. "Did you remember the spoon?"

Lexie facepalmed herself and went to the kitchen. She returned a minute later with a spoon for Emma.

"Thanks," Emma said sitting down next to her. "I was craving this like mad."

"Uh huh."

Emma glanced over at her and recognized the look of concern on her face. "I told him about the baby," she said softly. She sighed and slid a spoonful of ice cream into her mouth.

Lexie frowned, her eyes reading every inch of Emma's face as she waited for her to continue.

THE MISSING PIECE

"And it didn't go like I'd hoped," Emma said. She swallowed the lump in her throat and gave Lexie a half smile.

"It didn't? What happened? What did he say?"

Emma cleared her throat and placed the container of ice cream down on her nightstand. She zipped up her last piece of luggage and pushed it off the bed.

"I'm not going to go into everything he said, but in a nutshell, he dumped me."

"What?" Lexie gasped.

Emma nodded, watching her process the information. Lexie seemed just as shocked as she was when it happened. "I can't believe that, Em."

"He said he wasn't ready to be a father. He wanted me to get rid of it."

"Oh my God."

"Tell me about it."

"But I thought he had all these family values?"

"I thought so too, but it seems like that's not what he really wants. He said he'd be cool with it just being us, but he's not ready for a baby. So, he dumped me."

"Oh, Em." Lexie was at a loss for words, which didn't happen very often. "I was so sure he'd ask you to marry him. I'm sorry."

"It's all right. People leave me all the time. He's just one more."

Emma noticed that her statement had drawn tears in Lexie's eyes. She wasn't intending on making her cry, it just happened. This situation was just plain sad.

"What are you going to do now?" Lexie asked.

"What do you mean what am I going to do now?"

"I know people do it every day, but raising kids is hard."

Emma nodded. "It's hard, but worth it. At least this baby will grow up knowing that he or she belongs somewhere and with someone. That's the best gift you can give someone. A sense of belonging."

Lexie hugged her and grabbed the container of ice cream. "May I?"

"Help yourself," Emma said as she got up and pulled her bags into the living room. She returned and sat next to Lexie. She pulled a folder from her nightstand drawer and clasped it against her chest.

"What's that?"

Emma opened the folder, her head nodding slowly. "This is my pre-adoption birth certificate," she said handing it to her.

Lexie took it and scanned over the document. She glanced up at her, a frown creased her face. "But—"

"Yeah, I know," Emma interrupted.

"I thought you said that he found a name?"

"Didn't you say that a name was better than nothing?"

Lexie handed the document back to her. "But Jane Doe? What does that mean?"

Emma shrugged. "It could mean either they didn't know her name or this is the name she gave them when my birth certificate was filled out."

Lexie took the certificate and glanced over it again. "That's insane."

"Tell me about it."

"There's an address for her."

"Yep. I've already Googled it. I'm going to start my search there. Most likely, she's already moved on, but it's worth a try."

What she didn't tell Lexie was that the address listed as belonging to her birth mother was the address to a women's halfway house in Wyoming. She didn't want to speculate; she just wanted to wait and see, but the desire to find her real mother was stronger than ever. She needed to find her.

"When are you leaving?"

"I wanted to leave at sun-up, but that's not going to happen."

"How long of a drive is it?"

"Figuring in stopping to sleep, maybe a day or two."

"I hope you've planned to take many breaks."

"I'll see what I can do."

"Promise me, Em. I don't wanna have to worry the entire time you're gone."

"Okay. I'll take a lot of breaks."

"And you'll let me know when you get there safely?"

Emma groaned. "You're mothering me again, Lex."

Lexie laughed. "God, I'm sorry. I can't help it. If anything happens to you, I'll just die."

"Aww, that's so sweet, but stop being so extra."

They laughed. "But seriously, Em. Be smart and don't pick up any hitchhikers."

Emma gave her a quick salute and crawled under the covers. "I'm crashing. Lock up when you leave, all right?"

Lexie came around and tucked Emma in. "I'll crash on the couch so I can see you off later."

"Fine by me." Emma yawned and settled into her pillow. Thoughts of finding her mother swarmed around inside her head. She wondered what kind of person she would be and if she found her, would she have the courage to ask her the questions she desperately needed the answers to.

Emma had been on the road for nearly eight hours when she couldn't see to drive anymore. Her eyes burned, her back ached, and her head felt like there was a serrated knife sawing through her brain. She needed to stop immediately.

Her goal was to push through Iowa and stop somewhere in Nebraska. When she realized that she needed to stop, she was coming up on Sioux City. She'd almost made it to Nebraska. She gave herself credit for that.

She squinted to see the road sign coming up on her right. She was relieved to see decent hotels, restaurants, and stores on the sign.

She darted off the highway and pulled into the parking lot of the closest hotel. "I just need a little rest then I'll get back on the road. Just check in. Eat. Rest. That's it, Em."

She parked her car in a spot near the front of the hotel, repeating the list in her mind as she went inside.

Check in. Eat. Rest. That's it.

After she got the room keys, she went back to her car and grabbed her important items like the laptop, carry-on bag, and food. Her entire body buzzed from head to toe and her vision was blurred.

She couldn't remember a time when she was this tired. She stumbled into her hotel room, not even giving herself time to inspect it, and collapsed face down on the bed. She rolled over onto her back and placed her hand over her belly.

She must be more careful from here on out. She sighed and gazed at the ceiling. The room spun slowly as if she were on a slow-moving carousel. She closed her eyes. Check in. Eat. Rest. That's it.

"Must rest," she said with a yawn. She felt sleep overtaking her. She welcomed and needed it.

Her phone rang. Groaning, she turned it over to see who was calling. It was Lexie. She'd forgotten to return her call hours ago.

"Hi Lex, what's up?"

"Just calling to check on you."

"I'm good. I made it to a stopping point today. I'm at the hotel."

"I was worried when I didn't hear from you."

"There's no need to worry about me," Emma said, suppressing a yawn.

"Where are you staying for the night?"

"Sioux City."

"Holy crap!"

"Yep."

"You must've been breaking all kinds of speed limits."

Emma laughed softly and closed her eyes. It felt so good to close them. They didn't burn so much. "That's my secret."

THE MISSING PIECE

"Just be careful, you're carrying a kid now."

"I'm aware." Emma yawned loudly. "I'm beat, Lex. I'm going to call it a day."

Lexie sighed on the other end. "All right. Be safe, Em."

"Will do." Emma checked her messages. None. She tossed her phone onto the nightstand and turning off the lights. Her stomach ached and her head spun.

She probably should've eaten dinner before trying to sleep but sleeping was high on the priority list at the moment. She'd eat in the morning or whenever her body decided it'd had enough rest.

Until then... Rest. That's it.

The past two and a half days were just a blur. All Emma did was drive, sleep, and eat. And repeat. She'd done a cross country trip before, so she knew what to expect, but it was different this time. She was alone. It gave her a lot of time to think and plan ahead for what she was going to do once she found her mother. Something deep inside told her that she was going to find her. This gave her the confidence she needed to press forward.

Her heart raced when she came up on the road sign for Bridger, Wyoming. At her last stop, she did some research and found Bridger was small with a population just a little under 800. She thought it was great that there weren't that many people in town. But on the other hand, she knew smaller towns kept darker secrets.

First order of business was to find somewhere to stay. The only hotel in town didn't have online booking. When she pulled into the parking space in front of the hotel, her heart dropped into the pit of her stomach. It looked more like a roach motel than the 4-star hotel that the Internet said it was. She was too tired to worry about it.

She got out of her car and went inside. The lobby wasn't any better. It was stuffy and hot inside. She waited at the front desk for about five minutes before a clerk appeared.

"Good afternoon. Welcome to the Bridger Inn," he said. He was an older gentleman with a kind smile. Sweat dripped from his forehead over his pointed nose. "Let me guess, you need a room," he said with a laugh.

Emma offered a smile. "Yes. I need a room." She glanced around, not too sure if she wanted to stay here or not. "Unless you're booked up, then I could go to another hotel."

"Nonsense," he said, pulling out his guest registry. It looked to be a century old, thick and dusty. "We have plenty of space. Plus, we're the only inn for the next fifty miles."

"Are you serious?" she asked.

"Uh huh." He pulled a pen from behind his ear. "How many days you need?"

Emma sighed and glanced around once again. It wasn't anything like the places she was used to staying in, but it would have to do. "I'm not exactly sure. I'm here doing some research and I'm not sure how long it'll take."

He arched his brow and nodded. "Research, huh? Are you from the college?"

"No."

"The government? If you're from the government, I've paid all my taxes."

Emma laughed. "No. I'm here for personal research."

"Okay." He turned to a fresh page in his registry. "You'd have to pay in advance."

"That's no problem. How much are the rooms?"

"Depends on what you want."

"I'd like a comfortable bed, a tv, and bathroom with a hot tub if you have one." She knew he wouldn't have a bathroom with a hot tub, but it was funny to see his reaction.

"I can't help you with the jacuzzi, but I do have a spacious room with a king and a tv. We have satellite tv, so you'll get about two hundred channels. Or you can use the guest Wi-Fi to stream. I'll give you that room for one twenty a night. Is that good?"

"That's perfect. And I would like to stay for five days."

A smile crossed his face. "Five days it is," he said sliding the registry to her. "The room's all yours when you fill out your information here and prepay."

She quickly filled out her personal information on the form. She'd thought about giving an alias but then she thought better of it. This was a small record added in her journey to find her mother.

"Here you go." She slid the book back to him and smiled.

He looked over her information and nodded. "Chicago, huh?"

"Yes."

"You've come a long way to do research."

She nodded. "Yes, it's a personal project of mine. Family tree kind of stuff." She didn't want to give him too many details off the bat. If she needed to, she'd come back to him later with questions. But for now, she wanted to check in and find something to eat. She was starved.

"How do you wanna pay?"

She took out her card and slid it to him. "Just put it on there. If I need to stay longer, you can just use that."

He nodded and processed her card on the computer. "All done," he said. He retrieved a door key from the drawer and gave it to her. "We don't have fancy locks, so if you lose this one, you gotta pay to get another one."

"That's fair enough."

"And here's your card back. Room number twelve is yours. Go left out the door, your room is the last door before you turn the corner."

"Thanks." She gathered her paperwork and headed for the door. "Oh, could you tell me where a good place to eat is? I'm starved."

"Well, we only have the Tumbleweed Diner on the main strip. They have a little bit of everything there," he said.

"Thanks."

She went back to her car and grabbed her bags out of the trunk. Her body ached terribly. The last leg of the trip was brutal. Everything seemed to hurt. She found her room and went inside.

It was a nice, big room and it smelled clean and looked clean. That's all that mattered. She set up her laptop at the desk, took out her notepad and glanced over the notes she'd taken at her previous stop. It was going to be difficult tracking down her mother, but she was up for the challenge.

Typing in the last known address of her mother, she mapped it from the hotel. Surprisingly, it was only a two-minute drive. According to the directions, it sat on the opposite side of the street from the hotel. Next, she put in the name of the halfway house that popped up for the address.

According to the web, the Redemption Valley Halfway House was a place for women who'd been in trouble with the law and for women who had substance use disorders. It was founded in 1988, a nonprofit, and operated by two women.

THE MISSING PIECE

Emma scribbled down the names of the women who ran the halfway house and researched them. Betty and Nancy Richmond. Twin volunteers whose mission it was to help troubled women turn aside from their bad ways. They were heavy into the church and often hosted bingo parties and barbeques to raise money for their house.

Her stomach growled. She checked her watch. Time to eat. Now that she was off the road, she could get back to a better eating schedule. She opened up her messaging app on her laptop and sent Lexie a message.

Emma: I made it to my destination. Bridger, Wyoming.

The dots in Lexie's message box immediately started bouncing. Emma laughed to herself. Lexie must've been waiting for her text.

Lexie: That's great! You made great time. Thanks for letting me know.

Emma: You're welcome. I'll call you in a couple of days when I find something out.

Lexie: Awesome. Good luck, Em.

Emma: Thanks, I'm gonna need it. TTYL.

Lexie: Bye

Emma took a snapshot of a photo of the twin owners and closed her laptop cover. She was nervous, being in the town where it all began. She wondered if her mother was still here or if her search would take her elsewhere.

Even if she had to drive another thousand miles to find her, she would.

She gripped the side of the table as a wave of nausea washed over her. She cupped her stomach and waited for the feeling to pass. Eventually, she felt good enough to stand and she tested her balance before heading for the door. When she stepped outside, she looked toward the town center and spotted the diner. It was a short walk. The fresh air would do her good.

It was just her luck that the only place in town to order food had some of the worst options on their menu. She didn't recognize half the dishes being sold and she didn't feel like trying something new. She opted for a chicken Caesar salad just to be safe.

She waited patiently at the counter while the waitress cashed out her ticket.

"Do you take cards here?" Emma asked.

"No, I'm sorry. Cash only," the waitress said.

"Oh, I don't have any cash on me. I just assumed that credit cards were taken everywhere."

The waitress sighed and crossed her arms. "Are you passing through or are you new in town?"

THE MISSING PIECE

"I'll be here for a few days. I could run to an ATM really quick and get the money."

"The nearest ATM is in the next town over."

"How far is that?" Emma asked.

"About twenty miles."

"Yikes!"

The waitress laughed and scribbled something on Emma's ticket. "Listen, where are you staying?"

"At the Bridger Inn."

"Okay. I'll just keep this ticket open until I see you again. And I'll see you again because this is the only place to eat around here."

"Yes, I noticed," Emma said with a laugh.

"You can order what you want and when you're ready, just pay the balance."

"You'll do that for me?" Emma was surprised.

"Well, yeah, why not?"

"Because I don't even live here. How do you know I'm not going to take off and not pay?"

The waitress slid the ticket into the cash register and closed it. "I don't. I'm just hoping you won't do something like that. You don't look like the type."

Emma smiled at her. "I won't do that. I'll have some cash for that ticket the next time I come back, all right?"

"Sounds fine to me."

Emma turned to leave but turned back. "I'm in town doing some research. Do you mind if I ask you a question or two?"

"Make it quick."

Emma glanced down at her name badge and noted that her name was Victoria.

"People just call me, Vicks," the waitress said.

Emma was startled. It seemed like Victoria had read her mind. "All right, Vicks. Have you lived in Bridger long?"

"All my life," she answered.

Emma took a mental note of Victoria's appearance. She looked to be in her early thirties. She was most likely too young to be her mother.

"Do you know the Richmond twins?"

"Who doesn't? They are the most giving, kindest, and most loving people in this town. They've helped a lot of people. Including me."

"Do you know anything about Redemption Valley?"

Victoria's face sobered. "What do you need to know about it?"

"I just wanted some insight into the place. Do you know anyone who was a resident there?"

"I know a couple of girls who ended up there."

"What can you tell me about it?"

"I'm not sure what kind of information you're looking for, but all I know is that without the Richmonds and Redemption Valley, those girls would've been lost forever. They got the help they needed. That place was a godsend to the people who had to be there."

Emma nodded. "Thank you."

"No problem," she said, gesturing toward her other tables. "Gotta get back to work. See you later." She walked away before Emma could ask her anymore questions.

After eating what turned out to be a decent meal, Emma left the diner and headed back to her car. She second guessed her decision to walk the moment she set her feet to the pavement. Her ankles were aching terribly, and her knees felt weak. She was tired, exhausted from the long drive and needed at least a day's rest to recuperate.

The walk back seemed quicker. She jumped into her car and plugged the address to Redemption Valley into the navigation. It took her just two minutes to drive from the hotel to the halfway house. When she pulled up to the building her heart sank. It looked deserted and not a bit like the same place she found on the internet.

She got out of her car, walked up to the front door and peeked inside. It was dark and deserted. She looked at her watch. It was just a little after 4pm. If this place was open, there'd be people coming and going from the building. There wasn't a soul in sight.

"I can't believe this," she groaned.

She walked to the side of the building and peeked through the window. All she could see from that side was what seemed to be a dining area. Chairs were stacked on top of the tables and there was garbage on the floors. She walked around the back and peeked through the glass on the back door. She saw a long dark hallway. It was obvious that there wasn't any electricity being supplied to the building.

"Just great!" She'd driven all this way and the place wasn't even open.

She walked back to the front of the building and sat down on the front steps. She didn't know what to do next. Should she go back home? She leaned against the railing and closed her eyes. Tears stung the backs of them.

"Think, think," she encouraged herself. "This was unexpected, but it's not the end of the world, right?" She took a deep, stabilizing breath to calm herself. Finding this place empty triggered her negative thoughts.

She'd tried so hard to keep them quiet during the entire drive over. Now they were noisy and paralyzing. She should've known better than to come all this way in search of a woman who didn't want her in the first place.

"Excuse me, ma'am. Do you need some help?" a deep male voice asked.

Emma jumped and looked up. Standing in front of her was an officer in uniform. He stood taller than Cal, more muscular, too. He stepped closer, cautiously closing the distance between them.

"No, I just... I was looking for someone."

He glanced up at the building. "You were looking for someone here?"

"Yes. This was the only address I had. And I thought from the photos on the internet, the place was still open."

After a minute of silence, he slowly nodded his head. "Oh, I see. This place has been closed almost a year now."

"I should've called before I left home and made sure."

"Where is home?" he asked.

"Chicago."

"You came all the way from Chicago?"

"Yes."

"Who are you looking for?"

She hesitated to answer, but she knew she should answer his question. Maybe he could be of some help. "I'm looking for my mother. My birth certificate listed this place as her address."

He removed his sunglasses and motioned for her to stand up. "I need to see some identification."

"My purse is in my car."

"You may get it." He stepped aside and watched her walk to her car and retrieve her purse. She came back and handed him her driver's license. He took it and went back to his car. She didn't understand why he was running a check on her, but she went with it. After about ten minutes, he came back and handed her the license.

"Looks like you're safe."

"Of course, I'm safe. I'm just looking for someone."

"Well, you're in luck, Miss Benson."

"How so?"

He smiled and leaned against her car. "This place closed almost a year ago because they got bigger and built a place on the outskirts of town."

"Really?"

"Yes. The Richmonds bought some land and built a nice new place for the ladies out there."

"Wow, that's great. Could you tell me how to get there?"

He checked his watch. "The main office usually closes around three. So, you'll probably need to go first thing in the morning to talk to somebody."

Emma sighed heavily. She didn't like that answer one bit. "I really would like to talk to someone tonight. I'm anxious to find my mother."

"I understand that, but the people who could probably tell you what you're looking for aren't there now. If you'd like, I could drive you up there in the morning."

Emma groaned inside. She could use all the help she could get. "Listen, officer—"

"Deputy Sheriff Monroe," he said holding out his hand.

She took it and shook it quickly. "My apologies, Deputy Sheriff Monroe. I think I'll be fine. I'm just gathering information, that's all. I don't really need an escort."

He straightened up. "Are you sure? Because, there're plenty of places to get lost out there."

She laughed softly. "Yes, I'm sure. I found my way from Chicago, didn't I?" She smiled at him and hoped he would leave her alone.

He nodded. "All right," he said opening his notepad and scribbling down an address. He yanked off the page and handed it to her. "If you change your mind," he pulled a card from his shirt pocket. "Just give me a call."

She took it and glanced briefly at the card. Paul was his first name. "Thank you. I'll call you if I change my mind."

He tipped his hat, got into his car, and drove away. He didn't realize that he'd just saved her from melting into a pool of tears. He'd shown up at the perfect time. She slid his card into her back pocket and typed the new address into her phone. The estimated time to get to the new address was about ten minutes driving.

She got into her car and leaned her head against the steering wheel. She was extremely tired and needed rest, especially if she was going to go around asking questions in the morning. She started the car and headed back to the hotel.

Once there, she dragged herself into the room, stripped down, and got into the shower. The hot water relaxed her aching muscles as she leaned against the wall. She was overwhelmed with a new kind of emotion as she anticipated meeting someone who may have actually known her mother. After she was done with her shower, she crawled into bed, and fell fast asleep.

*E*mma waited nervously in the reception area. She'd been there for going on thirty minutes waiting for an opportunity to speak with Nancy Richmond. She'd picked the right day and time to visit because Nancy was on site today. Emma tried not to pick at her fingers, but her anxiety was through the roof. If this Nancy woman founded Redemption Valley, then most likely she knew her mother.

She took deep breaths and willed her heart to be steady. Sitting here this close to uncovering the truth was something that she'd dreamed about. Never did she imagine that she could be this close this soon.

"Miss Benson?"

Emma looked up to see the receptionist looking at her oddly. "Yes?"

"I said that Nancy will see you now."

"Oh!" Emma hopped to her feet. "Thank you." She followed the receptionist to the back of the office where she waited to be introduced. When invited, she walked in and took her seat in the guest chair in front of Nancy's desk.

She'd seen pictures of Nancy on the web, but she looked better in person. She had this glow about her. She was radiant. Nancy outstretched her hand and smiled at Emma.

"Good afternoon, how may I help you, Miss Benson?"

Where would she begin? Should she just unload everything all at once or should she just give her little bits and pieces and hope she'd remember the Jane Doe who gave birth to a child twenty-two years ago.

Emma shook Nancy's hand and sighed. "I was hoping you could help me find someone."

"Oh? Who are you looking for?"

Emma hoped that she'd found a receptive heart in this woman. Nancy Richmond looked warm and friendly. Kindness emitted from her smile and the softness in her eyes made Emma feel safe and comfortable. No wonder so many women took refuge with her.

"I'm looking for my mother."

"Your mother?"

"Yes. A few years ago, I found out that I was adopted, and when I became an adult, I was finally able to get my hands on my original birth certificate." Emma paused, trying to arrange the thoughts in her head so her words wouldn't spill out like a jumbled mess.

"Go on," Nancy said.

"The hospital didn't know her name, but the address to this halfway house was listed as her address?"

Nancy chuckled. "I'm sorry there must've been a mistake. We've only been at this address for a year."

"No, the original address off of Langley Drive. That's the address that I plugged into my GPS and went to and found out that it was closed. A policeman showed me how to find this place."

"I see," Nancy said leaning back in her chair. She adjusted her clothing and cleared her throat. "So, our old location on Langley was the address of the person you're looking for?"

"Yes."

"What's your mother's name?"

Emma pulled her birth certificate from her bag and slid it across the desk. "Well, I'm not really sure. I was hoping you could help me with that."

Nancy took it and examined it closely. Her forehead wrinkled into a frown. She glanced up at Emma before looking back down at the document. Emma saw her eyes move over each line of copy until she reached the bottom. She sighed and placed the paper down on her desk.

"Do you know who my mother is?"

"Yes, I knew her."

Emma's heart leaped inside of her chest. "Oh my God, really? You know my mother? Can you tell me about her?"

Nancy slid the certificate back to her. "Miss Benson, you must know that this is quite a surprise for me. This was so long ago."

"But you said you know her."

"True, but I'm not at liberty to give you personal details about her."

"I don't understand."

Nancy got up and walked over to the window. She stood there quietly gazing out the window for a few minutes before returning to her desk. She sat down with a heavy sigh.

"Yes, I knew your mother. She lived at Redemption Valley off and on."

"Lived? She was an addict?"

Nancy winced. "She struggled with an opioid use disorder. When she was here, she succeeded with our programs. But sadly, when she was released, she'd return later dependent on her preferred substances again."

Emma didn't really know what she expected but hearing that her mother was dependent on drugs put a damper on her excitement. "That's sad."

"She was such a determined young woman. She had a beautiful mind, but she was a tortured soul."

"Why are you referring to her in the past tense? Did she die?"

Emma succeeded in keeping the emotion out of her voice. She felt cold all over. For some reason, she thought she might meet her mother today and be able to see her in the flesh and hug her maybe. But that was out of the question now.

"No, she's not dead. I was just remembering the person I used to know."

"Oh."

"Redemption Valley was no place for a baby. Especially under the circumstances of your birth."

Emma swallowed hard. "What circumstances?"

Nancy sighed heavily. "Are you sure you want to know this information?"

"I drove all the way from Chicago to find my mother. Of course, I want to know."

"Okay. Well, sometime after she left Redemption Valley for a third time, she started using drugs again and also became pregnant with you. We hadn't heard from her in months, when one day I received a phone call from the sheriff informing me that she'd been arrested. When they booked her, she was under the influence of drugs and she was in active labor."

"Oh my God."

"She was rushed to the hospital and it was determined that the labor was premature."

"Are you kidding me?"

"No, I'm not. I went down to the hospital to be with her. I was responsible for her."

"So, my mother was high on drugs when she gave birth to me?"

"Yes."

"Unbelievable." Emma's stomach turned. "What about me?"

"You were so tiny and born addicted to opioids. We didn't think you'd make it."

Emma's mouth dropped open. "Opioids?"

Nancy nodded; a sympathetic expression crossed her face. "They didn't think you'd live through the night, but you did. The Child Protective Services stepped in and took custody of you."

"I... I can't believe this. I'm shocked."

"It was for the best. She was in no condition to take care of you."

Tears stung Emma's eyes. "I understand."

"I'm sorry, Miss Benson. I know you were probably expecting to hear something different."

"I really didn't know what I was expecting to hear, but it's nice to talk to someone who knew her."

THE MISSING PIECE

Nancy patted Emma on the hand. "Do you have any more questions?"

Emma nodded. "Did she want me?"

"Pardon me?"

"Did she want me?" she repeated. "Do you know if my mother wanted me?"

Nancy stared at her for a minute. "If it offers you any consolation, yes. She didn't know she was pregnant with you until she was admitted into the hospital. But when she found out, she wanted you, she just couldn't take care of you."

Emma held back her tears. "All right."

There was a knock on the door and Nancy called for the person to enter. Emma took the opportunity to gather her emotions. They were all over the place right now. She needed to get a grip.

A woman stepped in holding a stack of folders in her hand. She walked in talking and looking down at her tablet, completely unaware of the fact that Nancy was visiting with a guest.

"I've finished the onboarding interviews with the new residents, and they'll be ready for orientation by tomorrow. Do you want to grab lunch early? My treat."

When Nancy didn't respond, the woman looked up from her tablet and realized that Nancy was in the middle of a meeting.

"Oh, I'm so sorry!" she said. "I didn't know you had a guest." She placed the folders on the edge of Nancy's desk and backed away toward the door. "I'll come back."

"No worries, Jo," Nancy said gesturing towards Emma. "This is Emma Benson. Emma, this is Johanna Hauser. She is the Director of our sister facility, Charlotte's House."

"It's nice to meet you," Emma said taking Johanna's hand and shaking it. "What is Charlotte's House?"

"Charlotte's House is a sober living house for women who are recovering from addiction," Nancy replied.

All of this was new to Emma. She knew of drug addiction, but the Bensons kept her sheltered. The only true exposure she had was when she went to her first Cubs game as a teen and she saw a couple of men passing needles in the shadows of the stadium. It was foreign to her then, even more so now.

"I see," Emma said.

"Are you looking to join us?" Johanna asked.

"What? No, of course not! I'm not an addict." Emma realized from the look on her face that she'd offended her.

Johanna glanced over at Nancy, questioning her with a frown.

"Emma came all the way from Chicago in search of her long-lost mother." Nancy filled her in.

"Oh really?" Johanna said.

"Yes," Emma sighed. "My search began and ended here."

Nancy got up and joined Johanna. "Emma's mother used to be a resident here."

Emma rose from her seat and stuffed her birth certificate back into her bag. "Could you tell me where she is?" Emma asked.

Nancy walked Emma to the door. "I'm sorry, but I'm not at liberty to share that information with you."

"Can't you at least tell me her name? I know her name isn't Jane Doe."

Nancy shook her head. "She was listed as Jane Doe for a reason."

"What reason was that?"

Nancy shrugged and opened the door. "I'm sorry but—"

"You're not at liberty to share that information, right?" Emma's voice was filled with contempt. She was angry, not understanding why they couldn't tell her. She was a grown woman and had every right to know. "I came all this way to find my mother and I'm not going to let you, or your office policies stop me from finding out who she is."

"They're not just my office policies. It was for your own good that you were taken from her and adopted out."

"I need to know who she is. And I'm not leaving this town until I find out," Emma said.

Nancy nodded her head and gestured for Emma to leave. Even when she was dismissing her, she maintained her kind disposition. Emma had to find a way to get more information from her. Emma looked from Nancy to the stone-faced Johanna before she finally gave up and left the room. This was a lot to process.

Nancy closed the door behind Emma and sat down at her desk. Johanna sat across from her, watching her carefully.

"Who was that?"

Nancy slowly tapped her fingers on the desk. "I'm so glad I'm alive to see this. I knew she'd eventually find her way back home."

"Who was she?"

A smile crossed Nancy's face. "That young woman is Jane Doe's baby girl."

"What?" Johanna gasped. "That's impossible!"

"I saw the birth certificate. It's definitely her."

"But how do you know it's really her? That could have been anyone."

Nancy got up and walked over to the window. "She found her way back, Jo."

Johanna sighed and rose from her seat. She joined Nancy at the window and put her arm around her. "What are we going to do?"

"What's there to do?" Nancy asked.

"We could send her on a wild goose chase to get her as far away from here as we possibly can."

Nancy turned to her. "Why would we do that? She found her way home and came looking for her mother. Who are we to deprive her of that information?"

"It's a necessary evil," Johanna said.

"It was meant for her to come here."

"You can't get this girl's hopes up. Even if she's the baby all grown up, who's to say she doesn't have ulterior motives."

Nancy remained silent.

"You've been saving people all of your life, Nance. You've got to know when to stop."

Nancy spun around. "Every person that I've helped was lost and so is she. Why should I stop now when I've been waiting all these years for her to come back?" she asked.

"Do you hear yourself? We don't even know if she's who she says she is!"

"I know she's who she says she is!" she snapped back.

"How do you know for sure?"

"Because when she sat down across from me and looked into my eyes, I saw her mother." She let the words sink in before continuing. "I saw the same person who came to me for help when she had nowhere else to go. And I can't turn her away."

"You can't tell her what you've sworn you'd never tell, Nance."

"I know. I know." Nancy went back to her desk and opened her laptop. "I don't plan on telling her anything, she'll have to uncover the truth herself."

Johanna crossed her arms and gazed out of the window. "Do you think she'll start digging on her own?"

"Absolutely. She's here, isn't she?"

"We can't let her uncover the truth."

"Our control is limited, Jo. You should've seen the fire in her eyes. It was amazing."

Johanna turned and looked at her. "You sound like you want to tell her everything."

Nancy sighed and gestured for Johanna to come and sit by her. Johanna pulled up a chair and sat. Nancy took Johanna's hand and smiled at her.

"You know how I felt about that little baby when she was born, don't you?"

"Yes."

"When she walked in today, and before I even laid eyes on that birth certificate, I knew she'd come home."

"But how? I don't understand how you could know it."

Nancy squeezed Johanna's hand. "Jo, listen to me."

"I'm listening."

"Only a handful of people know about Emma. I wanted it that way for a reason."

Johanna gazed into her eyes. "Because you knew she'd return one day?"

"Yes. And I didn't want the mistakes of the past to impede her finding her way back to her family. I got to spend that little time watching her and talking to her through the incubator glass. I would've given anything to hold her in my arms."

Johanna's expression softened and a smile creased the corner of her mouth.

"I'm a woman of prayer. I prayed for her to be watched over, and I asked if one day she could find her way back home to us. And my prayer was answered today."

Johanna nodded but didn't say anything in response. "Once she finds out the true identity of her mother, she's not going to want anything to do with her."

Nancy shrugged. "You could be wrong. Time heals everything."

Silence fell over them, each woman keeping to her own thoughts. Johanna leaned back in her chair. "Do you think she'll show up at the House?"

"Most likely," Nancy said.

"What do I do then?"

"Then you just answer whichever questions you're comfortable answering. And let her draw her own conclusions."

"I don't know about this, Nance."

"Let me ask you this. When you woke up today what kind of day did you think you were going to have?"

Johanna shrugged. "I don't know. A normal one, I guess."

"Me too. But Emma woke up this morning probably thinking she was going to find out more information about her mother than she actually did. Can you imagine how she feels?"

"No, I can't."

"She's already told me that she's not going anywhere until she gets answers. It's not going to take her long to figure it out if the apple didn't fall too far from the tree."

Johanna shook her head slowly.

"We can't stop what's happening, Jo. We can't stand in the way. She needs to know."

"I know she does."

"When she comes asking, tell her what she needs to know, okay?"

Johanna tightened her jaw, hesitating briefly before nodding in agreement. "All right. I'll tell her whatever she needs to know."

"Thank you."

"I hope you're right about this, Nance."

Nance patted her on the hand. "I am," she said with a smile. "Do you still want an early lunch?"

"You bet I do."

"Great. Let's go."

They said nothing else on the topics of Jane Doe or Emma. They'd spent the last two decades making sure Jane Doe's secret remained unknown, but Emma's arrival threatened to change it all.

Emma leaned against the wall and inhaled a deep breath. Hopefully this was the last time she'd have to vomit. She'd nothing left in her stomach. She was dizzy and her stomach ached. The room spun slowly around her. She groaned and pulled herself to her feet. There was a light knock on the stall door.

"Excuse me, miss. Do you need some help?"

Emma felt a mixture of gratitude and irritation as she took another deep breath. "No, I'm okay. Just morning sickness," she said. Although she'd never been pregnant before, this didn't feel right.

She shook the negative thoughts from her mind and straightened up in the stall. She flushed the toilet and tested her balance again. Her legs were steady enough to stand up straight. She opened the stall door and stepped out.

THE MISSING PIECE

The woman stood by the door with a sympathetic expression on her face. "I'm sorry. I know how that is. I have five myself."

Emma smiled. She wasn't really interested in chit chat at the moment. She put one foot in front of the other and made her way to the sink. She turned on the water, splashing cool water over her face before rinsing out her mouth. After drying her face, she smiled at the woman and shrugged.

"I guess I'll get used to it, huh?" she said.

"How far along are you?"

"Just a couple of months," Emma guesstimated as she made her escape out of the bathroom. She sat at the high counter and ordered a warm drink. She didn't have an appetite. She kept thinking about the news that she was born addicted to drugs.

She pulled out her phone and searched up opioid addictions. Her skin flashed cold as she read a list of drugs that her mother could've been addicted to.

Vicodin. Morphine. Hydrocodone. Heroin.

She half wondered which one or ones Jane Doe was addicted to. "Why didn't she give them her real name?" she said out loud. "Was she so out of it that they couldn't get a name from her or did she deliberately refuse to give them her real name?"

Her mind again replayed the conversation with Nancy. "Nancy seemed to know who she was..." Emma took a sip of the tea that was put in front of her. "If the police called Nancy and if Nancy knew who she was the entire time then most likely Nancy knows her real name..." She sighed and took another sip of tea. "So why all the secrecy?"

"What secrecy are you referring to?" said a voice behind her.

She spun around to see Deputy Monroe smiling at her. "Oh my God, you scared me," she said.

"Sorry, miss," he said tipping his campaign hat.

"Do you make it a habit of going around scaring visitors?"

He shrugged. "Well that depends on my mood." He sat on the barstool beside her and removed his hat. The waitress appeared in front of him.

"Hi, Paul, do you want the usual?" she asked.

"You got it, Vicks." He said, flashing her a smile. She chuckled and walked away only to return a minute later with a fresh cup of black coffee. He took it and drank it slowly while he read the paper.

Emma looked over at him and wondered if she should engage him in conversation. She'd need his help if Nancy continued to refuse to give her answers. He caught her looking at him out of the corner of his eye. He nodded and smiled at her.

"How's your day, Deputy?"

"It's going well so far. It's slow today, but—" the chatter from his shoulder radio caught his attention. He listened, and then spoke a confirmation back to the dispatcher. "But I expect it to liven up here soon enough."

"That's good."

"How's your search coming along?"

"Okay, I guess. I spoke to Nancy but I hit a roadblock."

"Oh?"

"Yes, she knows my mother, but she won't give up her name. So, I'm going to have to find that out somehow on my own."

"Hmm," was all he said.

Emma found it strange that he didn't ask any more questions. He looked old enough to know secrets. Being a Deputy Sheriff, no doubt he knew the secrets of every resident here. His face had blanked, his smile had disappeared. She didn't know if she could trust him, but she had nothing to hide.

"I just wish she would've told me her name," Emma said.

"I'm sure she has her reasons. Nance is a pillar in the community. She's helped a lot of people."

"So, I've been told."

He grabbed his hat and toyed with the rim. "Do you think your mother still lives here?"

"I think so, but I just need to find out who she is first, then I can go from there."

He nodded. "As long as you don't go around pissing people off, you can poke around and see if you can find her."

"Thank you, Deputy Monroe."

He stared at her for a long minute before nodding slowly. "Just call me Paul."

Emma smiled. "All right, Paul. Thank you very much."

He slipped on his hat and stood. "If you run into any problems, just let me know and I'll see if I can help."

"Thanks again."

"You're welcome, Miss Benson. I hope you find her." He tipped his hat and then left the diner.

As she watched the door close behind him, she couldn't stop thinking about her conversation with Nancy Richmond. Nancy probably knew every detail there was to know, and Emma realized that perhaps the Deputy knew something, too.

8

Emma jotted down the address of the town clinic on her notepad. She needed to get checked out by a doctor to ease her worries. The drive to Bridger was hard on her back and maybe that's why she was experiencing the level of discomfort that she was feeling at the moment.

Her phone rang. She groaned and cursed under her breath when she realized it was Ericka calling. "Hey, Mom, what's up?"

"How are you?" Ericka asked.

Emma frowned at the phone. "I'm fine. How are you?"

"I'm doing well today. Are you busy at the moment?"

Emma transferred the phone to the other ear and continued researching on the computer. She needed a distraction. Every time she and Ericka had a conversation, she always ended up angry. Ericka must've expected her to reach out for money by now.

"Just surfing the web. What's going on?" Emma said.

"I'd like to know where you are."

"Why?"

"Because I think it's wise to let someone know your whereabouts just in case something happens to you."

"Are you expecting something to happen to me?"

"Of course not, Emma. Don't be ridiculous."

A period of silence followed. Emma occupied herself by doing further research on Redemption Valley. They'd received high ratings and overwhelmingly positive reviews. The Richmonds apparently ran the place very well.

She found an article dated three years ago about the grand opening and dedication of Charlotte's House. "Charlotte's House, hmm," she mused.

"Excuse me?" Ericka said.

Emma momentarily forgot that Ericka was on the other line. "Oh, sorry, Mom. I'm just doing some research."

"What kind of research?"

"Personal."

"Why are you being so secretive, Emma?" Ericka's voice was void of emotion as usual. "What are you hiding?"

Emma sighed. "I'm not hiding anything. There just comes a point in a person's life when they just want to be alone. That's where I am right now."

"You haven't called in days."

"If I remember correctly, you told me that I was on my own," Emma said.

She knew what Ericka was doing. She wasn't genuinely concerned. She was just calling to make sure that Emma wasn't running around bringing shame on the Benson name again.

"Make sure you bring yourself home in one piece, please. We have the fall gala at the Sears Tower coming up and I'd like for you to be present."

Emma chuckled. "Don't you mean the Willis Tower, Mom? You can't stroke the egos of the English donors if you keep calling it Sears."

Ericka sighed. "It'll always be the Sears Tower to me, Emma. When necessary, I'll refer to it by its proper name."

Of course, Ericka couldn't take a joke. "All right. Yes, I'm aware of the gala and I'll be back home before then."

"Thank you," Ericka said. "I should be going now."

"All right. Goodbye."

"Goodbye, Emma."

When Ericka disconnected the line, Emma felt a familiar ache in her chest that she always felt when she got off the phone with her. At least this time it didn't hurt so much. Maybe knowing that she was in the same town as her mother eased her pain. Whatever it was, she was thankful for it.

She turned her attention back to the computer screen where she continued to read the article about Charlotte's House. Many important people turned out for its dedication. The Richmond twins know some pretty important people. The article mentioned that even the Governor of Wyoming had attended.

"Pretty impressive," she said to herself.

She clicked on the company profile and read more about the Richmond twins. The extent of their philanthropic activities impressed her. She thought Ericka was good, but Nancy and Betty Richmond were better.

She saw a picture of the woman from Nancy's office, the director, and clicked on her profile. Her biography described her as a dedicated, business-minded individual with a heart of gold. It further described her as a nature and horse lover who was also a team player, always looking out for the interests of others. Emma gazed at her photo for a moment.

The woman she met at the office today seemed stand-offish and overprotective. Emma could tell during the brief encounter earlier that the woman didn't trust her. It was all in the way she looked at her, although her profile photo painted a different picture. Emma scribbled down some notes and went on to the next staff member, and then the next.

THE MISSING PIECE

The more she read about the women working at Charlotte's House the more her curiosity was piqued. The common denominator between each one the members is that they all either worked or resided at Redemption Valley at one point in time. One of them had to know something about her mother.

Deep down Emma had a feeling that the answers lie with either Redemption Valley or with Charlotte's House. She just didn't know which one. She checked her watch.

"It's late enough in the day, maybe I can catch someone in a good mood."

She glanced down at her handwritten notes. As long as she didn't violate the rights of the residents, she could ask any questions she wanted. The Deputy said so himself. Without further hesitation she left the hotel. Next stop, Charlotte's House.

She arrived at Charlotte's House a little before 4 p.m. The main house was in the style of a rustic mountain lodge. There were so many windows that Emma lost count of them. The cobblestone driveway circled a large stone fountain in the center of the property.

Behind the main house was the most beautiful view of a mountain range that Emma had ever seen. From town, she could see the mountains, but from here they seemed like they were literally in the backyard. The property was absolutely breathtaking.

She was thankful to find the front doors of the lobby still open. She went inside, taking mental notes of how luxurious the lobby and main reception area was. Her eyes couldn't resist being drawn to the chandelier above the receptionist station. From what she'd seen already, the Richmonds had probably spent a few million dollars on building and decorating a place like this.

"Good afternoon," Emma said leaning against the front desk.

"Good afternoon, how may I help you?" asked the front desk clerk.

THE MISSING PIECE

Emma glanced down at her name badge. She wasn't one of the women that she'd read about online. "Hi, yes. I'd like to speak with Johanna Hauser, please."

"Do you have an appointment?" she asked.

"No, I don't. Do I need one?"

The receptionist nodded. "Are you here about residency?"

"No. I just need to speak with her about something else." Emma leaned in closer. "It's a little personal."

The receptionist shook her head slowly. Eventually she picked up the phone. "What's your name, please?"

"Emma Benson."

"One moment, Miss Benson." She dialed Johanna's extension and waited for her to answer. "I'm sorry to bother you, Johanna, but there's someone here to see you." The receptionist glanced up at her and smiled. "Her name is Emma Benson."

Emma waited patiently for the receptionist to finish her conversation. She looked around, catching sight of a blond woman who resembled one of the women on the website. She was almost certain it was her. The receptionist hung up the phone.

"I'm sorry, Miss Benson, but Johanna isn't available at the moment, but if you'd like to wait, she'll be free in about thirty minutes."

"Sure, that's fine," Emma said. She was happy that the lady agreed to speak with her, she didn't care if she had to wait.

"You can stay here in the lobby or feel free to walk around outside."

"What time do you close your lobby?"

"We close at 5:30 p.m."

Emma noticed the familiar woman walk outside through the double doors. "Great. I think I'll walk around outside. It's a beautiful day."

"It certainly is. Remember to come back in thirty minutes. Johanna is very busy, and you might miss your opportunity."

"Will do, thank you." Emma followed the same path as the blond woman, stepping outside and into the courtyard separating the main house and four smaller cabin houses.

It seemed like she'd stepped into another world, a paradise-like garden. From the driveway, this area of the property was unseen, but it was such a nice surprise. She might be able to reach out and touch the mountain range in the background. It was that close.

A couple of women were sitting on a bench by another fountain laughing and talking. Up on the hill two horses walked around inside their fenced-in enclosure. Emma was far away from Chicago, but oddly this place felt like home.

While she was admiring the beauty of her surroundings, she lost sight of the blond lady. She couldn't have gone far. Emma walked down the cobblestone path toward the glistening lake. It drew her in like a lighthouse welcomes a ship into its harbor.

Mesmerized, she walked down to the dock and stood against the railing. She inhaled a deep breath. The air was so fresh, fresher than anything she'd ever smelled before. She reached out, laughing to herself when she couldn't quite touch the mountains in front of her.

"They look like you can almost touch them, don't they?"

She spun around, nearly tripping over her own feet. Emma had been so focused on the lake that she didn't even notice that she'd walked past Johanna sitting in the gazebo. Her cheeks heated up with embarrassment.

"You scared the crap out of me," Emma said.

Johanna laughed and looked back down at her book. "Well, I'm sorry."

"They told me you weren't available," she said walking closer to her.

"Because I'm not. I'm on a short break."

"Do you mind if I sit next to you?"

"This gazebo is big enough for the both of us," Johanna answered. She looked at Emma from over the top of her book. "Sit anywhere you like."

"Thank you." She took a seat right next to her. This is one of those times she wished they were in or close to Chicago. She'd definitely be able to use the Benson influence to get the answers she needed. This one here seemed like she was going to be a hard one to crack.

"What brings you to Charlotte's House, Emma?" Johanna asked.

Emma knew that Johanna probably wanted to get rid of her as quickly as possible. She had that look about her, so she decided to get straight to the point. "As you know, I'm searching for my mother."

Johanna nodded. "Yes. How can I help you?"

"May I ask you a few questions, please? It would really help in my search."

"What're you hoping to find out?" Johanna asked, placing her book on her lap.

"I came all this way with hopes of finding out if she's alive and Nancy confirmed that she is. So now, I just want to know who she is and maybe where she lives."

Johanna remained silent. Emma wondered who Jane Doe was and why everyone was guarding her identity so closely.

"I read your bio online," Emma said.

"It needs updating."

Emma smiled. "It was great. Impressive."

"What kind of questions do you have, Emma?" she said glancing at her phone.

"Your bio said that you were with Redemption Valley before you came to work here."

"Yes, that's true. Three of us came over from Redemption. The three of us who'd been with Nance longest were used to establish a base of credibility here at Charlotte's House."

"Three of you?"

"Yes. Tanisha, Maggie, and I. We've been with Nance since ninety-six."

"Wow, that's a long time."

"Certainly is." Johanna adjusted herself in the seat and cleared her throat. "Charlotte's House is a home for the residents. A safe haven."

"Yeah. I read that on the website." Emma watched her briefly. Johanna held her eye contact, never once blinking or looking away. "Did you know Jane Doe? Did you know my mother?"

"Yes, I knew her."

"Could you tell me why her identity is such a secret? I mean, was she, like, important or something?"

Johanna got up and walked over to the railing. "She was just a regular girl. She had a lot of issues that caused her to relapse whenever she left Redemption."

"Nancy told me about some of them. Why was it so hard for her?"

Johanna gazed out across the lake. "I'm guessing because she didn't have support on the outside. She did great inside. She was safe. She was loved." Her voice trailed off as she watched the ripples in the water.

"So, she couldn't handle the pressure in the real world?" Emma asked.

"I guess it's something like that. Her only support system was Redemption, but the bad thing about that was that you couldn't stay at the halfway house for a long period of time. You had to recover and leave."

"Nancy said that my mother was a resident off and on."

"Yes, she was."

"How many times did my mother stay at the halfway house?"

"I don't know. I lost count."

Emma moved closer to her. She discerned that Johanna was receptive enough to ask a few more questions. She needed to make them count. "Could you please tell me what her name is?"

Johanna shook her head. "I can't, I'm sorry."

"I don't understand," Emma said. "Why can't you tell me?"

Instead of responding, Johanna looked in the other direction. Emma leaned against the railing next to her and thought about what she'd say next. She needed to keep the lines of communication open. This woman knew more than she was letting on.

"Do you have a mother?" Emma asked.

"She's passed away."

"When she was alive, what did it feel like to be hugged by her?"

Johanna inhaled deeply. "It was the best feeling in the world."

"The woman who adopted me never gave me affection. She rarely hugged or kissed me. Whenever I was scared, she'd tell me to get over it. I was a charity kid, you know."

Johanna turned and looked at her. She frowned but said nothing.

"I want to know what that feels like. Can't you understand that?"

Johanna nodded.

"It brings me so much comfort knowing that she wanted me, but she just couldn't take care of me. I get that. And maybe if I find her, I can tell her what I need to tell her."

"What do you need to tell her?"

"I want to tell her that I understand, and that I forgive her." Emma paused to collect her thoughts. "I want to show her that I'm alive and—" she sighed heavily and dropped her head.

"And what?"

Emma wasn't sure if telling her would make a difference, but she wanted this woman on her side. If she could convince Johanna to tell her who her mother was, she wouldn't need to dig so deep.

Emma wrung her hands in front of her. "I want an opportunity to tell her that I'm having a child of my own."

"You are?"

Emma nodded. "I need the closure, even if she wants nothing to do with me, I need to know that I found the person I've been searching for."

"Everyone needs closure."

Emma saw that she'd gained some of Johanna's trust. Johanna's face had softened, her body more relaxed.

"And I thought she might need closure too," Emma added.

Johanna turned toward the lake. "You look a lot like her."

"I do?"

"Nance said that when she looked into your eyes, she saw her. I see it now too."

"You have no idea how good that makes me feel."

"Nance knew you'd show up here asking questions. She told me you would," she said turning to face her.

Emma laughed. "I'm not sure if that's good or bad."

"My break is over." She walked up the pathway towards the main house. "How long will you be in town?"

Emma hurried to catch up to her. "Until you guys get sick of me, I guess."

Johanna chuckled. "Don't you work?"

"I do, but I took a leave of absence until I sort through my personal issues."

"I see." Johanna kept an unhurried pace, taking the time to stop and talk to different residents along the way.

Emma noticed how much the people respected her. She dealt with each person in a kind and loving way. She greeted each woman with a hug, a warm smile, and a compliment. Nothing about Johanna was practiced. Everything she did came straight from her heart.

Emma found herself smiling as she watched her interact with the women. And then the blond woman approached them. She greeted Johanna with a simple nod and then sized Emma up in a matter of seconds.

"Hey, Mags. How's your day going?" Johanna said.

"Sucks," Maggie said.

Johanna laughed a little. "What's wrong now?"

"You're working me to death, that's what's wrong. I literally just finished updating the software on the computers when you added more work to my queue!"

Johanna glanced over at Emma and shook her head. "You're the smartest member of our team, Mags. Who else am I going to get to make sure our technology is working properly?"

"Uh, hello! What about Tanisha? She just got back from vacation and I need one."

Johanna laughed and put her arm around her. "I promise you'll get your vacation soon. We just need to make sure everything is working properly before the fundraiser barbeque this weekend."

"Come on, Jo," Maggie groaned. "I'm working on fumes."

Johanna sighed and pulled her in closer. "Okay, how about this. If you finish running the diagnostics on the servers, you can take tomorrow off and have a three-day weekend. How does that sound?"

Maggie thought about it for a minute. "Sounds like you've got yourself a deal."

"Thanks, Mags."

"No problem." Maggie turned her attention back to Emma when Johanna stood beside her. "Is this a new resident?" she asked.

"I was getting around to introducing you two. Emma this is Maggie, our Technology Director."

Emma shook Maggie's hand. "It's nice to meet you, Maggie. I read your profile online."

"Did you now?" she said with a laugh. "What did you think of it?"

"Impressive," Emma said. "Your social media is even more impressive."

A smile crossed Maggie's face. "Well, thank you."

Johanna cleared her throat. "Mags, this is Emma Benson. She's visiting Bridger for a while. She's searching for her mother."

"Oh really? Someone I know?"

"Yes. Jane is her mother," Johanna replied.

Emma had never in her life seen the color fade from someone's face so quickly. Maggie's reaction made her even more curious about the secrets surrounding her mother.

"Wow," was all Maggie said in reply.

"Did you know my mother?"

Maggie nodded and stepped away from them. "Yep, I sure did."

"Could you tell me anything about her? What was she like?"

Maggie looked at Johanna. Johanna nodded, giving her the go head.

"Back then she was the most stubborn and most obnoxious woman that I'd ever met. Every single day she irritated me to no end," she said with a laugh. "But she was real. She was as real as real gets. And she's still like that today."

"You're still friends with her?"

Maggie nodded. "We talk every day."

"Wow," Emma whispered. She was staring into the eyes of her birth mother's closest friend it seemed. She was getting warmer in her search. "I can't believe your friendship has lasted all these years."

Maggie shrugged. "Not many things could get in the way of our friendship. The only thing that tested it was when she'd disappear on me for months at a time. I'd just have to trust that she knew where home was."

"Where was home?"

"Home was with us." Maggie held Emma's gaze for a while. "I'll tell you this one thing."

"What?"

"If you've got it in your head that you're gonna come out here and give her a piece of your mind, then you might as well forget it." Maggie stepped further away and shoved her hands into her pockets. "People experience things so painful that they can't ever talk about it without reopening the wound. That's her. When she lost you, she was completely broken." The words faded from Maggie's lips as if they were too painful to say.

"I... I didn't know?"

"Yeah, well now you do. This is a fair warning. If you come out here and hurt her, you'll have to deal with me."

Emma swallowed hard and nodded. "Okay. How do I find her?"

Maggie put a hand on her shoulder and squeezed it gently. "If I could, I'd tell you who she is right now."

"Why can't you?"

"Because she's my friend and I love her. And I don't want to overstep."

Emma lowered her head, cursing under her breath. "I don't understand why everyone is protecting her from me. It's not like I'm going to disrupt her life. I just want to meet her."

"We understand that," Maggie said.

"If you understood, you guys wouldn't do this to me. I've counted three people who know her very well, but who won't tell me a damn thing about her. I just want to see her. Can't you understand that?"

Maggie sighed and looked over at Johanna. "Hey, Jo, why don't we invite Emma to dinner tonight?"

"What?" Johanna said.

"How does that sound, kid?" Maggie asked.

"Dinner? I don't know."

"We can talk more about this. We all can." Maggie said.

Emma noticed Johanna glaring at Maggie. The two women exchanged an unspoken dialogue before Johanna nodded in agreement.

"Yes, that's a great idea. Please join us for dinner, Emma," Johanna said calmly.

Emma's gaze bounced from Johanna to Maggie several times before she finally agreed.

"Dinner sounds great."

"Perfect!" Maggie said before backing away. "I'll see you two this evening. I gotta go work on those servers so I can get the weekend off." And then she was gone. She disappeared so quickly Emma wondered if she'd been there in the first place.

An awkward silence settled between them. Emma laughed to fill in the gap of conversation. "I'm sorry, I'm a little stunned," Emma said.

"Understandably."

"I don't have to come for dinner tonight. I can tell you don't really want me to."

"Nonsense."

Emma laughed. "I saw the way you looked at her. It doesn't take a rocket scientist to realize that you don't want me around."

Johanna shot her a look that made her want to crawl into a shell. Emma was learning that this woman had many layers to her. Johanna stared at her without saying a word before she laughed and continued up the hill. Emma followed closely behind.

"You're a smart young woman, Emma, but you're wrong about that one. I was just surprised that she'd invited you, that's all. I haven't had time to clean our house yet."

"You two live together?"

"Yes, we're roommates. The house belongs to her, but I rent out the top level."

"That's pretty cool. You two seem close."

Johanna glanced at her sideways. "We are. I'm one of her best friends, but she'll never admit that."

Emma chuckled. "That's cool. I have a best friend. She acts like I'm her child."

"Don't they all."

"Lex would totally love it here. She likes wide open spaces."

"Well, perhaps you should bring her back here one day," Johanna said.

"That's a great idea. That is if everything goes smoothly when I find my mother. If this town is as small as it seems, I'm surprised I haven't run into her by now."

Johanna stopped at the top of the hill. She looked toward the horse enclosure and whistled. Emma was surprised that such a loud sound could come from a person. A minute later, she heard the sound of heavy footsteps galloping toward them. She turned and saw a beautiful brown horse approaching them.

The horse slowed and stopped in front of Johanna. "Hey, girl," she cooed, caressing the horse's silky golden mane. "We have a visitor today."

The horse looked at Emma. She neighed and nodded her head as if she understood what Johanna had said.

"Wow, did you teach her to do that?" Emma asked.

Johanna chuckled. "I wish. She's a smart girl."

"May I touch her?"

"Sure." Johanna guided the horse over and positioned her in front of Emma. "Her name is Astrid. She's mine."

Emma reached out and caressed the horse's nose. Astrid bumped Emma's hand with her nose and neighed softly.

"I'd say she likes you," Johanna said.

"She's absolutely beautiful."

"Thank you. Our residents favor her over Wolfgang," she said tipping her head toward the other horse. "He belongs to Mags. He's just like her. He bullies everyone."

Emma chuckled and stroked her fingers through Astrid's hair. "I love her coloring. My adoptive mother had a horse, but I was never able to touch him."

"Oh? What kind?"

Emma shrugged. "I'm not even sure. He was huge though."

"You're more than welcome to visit with Astrid as much as you like. She's very friendly and it seems like she enjoys your company as well."

Astrid bumped Emma on the cheek and sniffed her hair, soliciting a giggle from both Emma and Johanna. Johanna tugged the horse over.

"All right, girl. Leave our guest alone. Time to go back," she said clicking her teeth and patting the horse lightly on the backside. They watched the horse run back into the enclosure, where she went back to grazing.

"She's amazing," Emma said.

"Thanks. I've had her ever since she was a yearling."

"What happened to her mom?"

"Astrid was rescued along with her mother from an unauthorized breeder, but her mother was severely malnourished and died a few days later."

"Aww."

"Yes, it's very sad."

"So, you were like her adoptive mother, huh?"

Johanna smiled and opened the door. "Yeah, I guess you can say that."

"You've done an amazing job. She looks very healthy and happy."

"Thank you."

Emma followed Johanna inside where they gathered by the coffee station. "This place is really nice. It's peaceful here," Emma said.

"Thanks. We try to make it as nice as possible here for our residents. We have outdoor activities in the spring and summer and arts and crafts in the fall."

"I don't know much about addiction, but it seems like the people are happy here."

"I believe they are," Johanna said. "At least I haven't heard any complaints yet." She poured a cup of coffee and sipped it slowly. "Would you like something to drink?"

"No, I'm okay. Thanks though."

"How does seven sound for dinner?"

"Seven is good," Emma said with a smile.

Johanna jotted down her address on a napkin and handed it to her. "If you have no other questions, I really need to get back to work."

THE MISSING PIECE

Emma admired Johanna's handwriting. She crossed her sevens and slashed her zeros just like she did. "No, I'm good for now. You've been very helpful. I really appreciate it."

"All right. I'll see you this evening," Johanna said. She took her coffee and headed back to her office.

Emma watched her leave. She was thankful that she'd misjudged her at first. Johanna could turn out to be an ally if she played her cards right. At least that's what she hoped. Without wasting another minute, she left the House and headed back to town. She had a dinner to prepare for.

Johanna hadn't spoken a word to Maggie since she got home. Thanks to Maggie's spur-of-the-moment invitation, Johanna had to rush home, clean up, and prepare dinner. She had planned on working on her painting when she got home, but now that was out of the question.

She busied herself in the kitchen, avoiding Maggie's gaze whenever she came close. It was unlike her to give Maggie the silent treatment, but what she'd done was unacceptable.

"Would you talk to me, Jo?" Maggie asked.

Johanna stirred the rice on the stove one more time before turning around. "We don't have anything to talk about."

"Why are you giving me the cold shoulder?"

"I'm not."

"You haven't said two words to me since I got home."

"And?"

"I want to know why," Maggie said.

Johanna noticed that her hands were trembling, so she hid them in her apron pockets and leaned against the counter.

THE MISSING PIECE

Maggie got up and walked over to her. "Why are you shaking? Are you okay?"

"I'm fine."

Maggie pulled Johanna's hands from her pockets and held them. "I said are you okay?"

Johanna moved away from her. "And I said that I'm fine."

"Why are you shaking?" she repeated.

Johanna laughed and yanked her apron off and tossed it on the counter. She turned the burner down and let the rice simmer. "Maybe because I'm nervous," Johanna admitted.

"About the kid coming?"

"Yes, about the kid coming! Why'd you do this?"

"Why not?"

Johanna left the kitchen and plopped down on the sofa. "Why not? Because it wasn't your place to invite her, Mags. What were you thinking?"

"I just put myself in her shoes. She needs to know the truth, Jo. It's cruel giving that kid the runaround when we've got the answers right here."

Johanna shook her head slowly.

"Do you think it's a coincidence that she showed up now?"

"I don't know," Johanna whispered. "I don't know what to think about this."

"Nance had me do some checking on her."

"And what did you find out?"

Maggie sat down beside her and propped her feet up on the coffee table. "Let's just say, the kid doesn't need anything from us."

"What does that mean?"

"Apparently the people who adopted her are important people in Chicago. She's not after money."

"Then what does she want?"

"Seems like she just wants her mother, Jo," Maggie said. "I think that's all she wants," she said a little softer.

Johanna wrung her hands and sighed heavily. "Are you sure?"

"I'm almost certain."

Johanna glanced at the clock. Emma would be arriving in twenty minutes. Her forehead beaded with sweat. She tugged at her shirt collar, releasing the tension that'd built up inside of her.

"She's going to be interrogating us again, you know that, right?" Johanna said with a laugh.

"The apple doesn't fall too far from the tree on that one."

They both laughed. "She's going to be disappointed when she finds out," Johanna's voice was just above a whisper, but Maggie heard her.

"I doubt it." Maggie reached over and covered Johanna's trembling hands with her own. "It'll be okay, Jo. I promise."

"I hope you're right."

"She just wants answers. Just start there."

The doorbell rang. Johanna jumped in her seat. Of course, Emma would arrive early for dinner. She should've guessed. She got up quickly and smoothed out her shirt. She looked at Maggie and shrugged.

"You look great," Maggie reassured her.

Johanna nodded and hurried to the door. She opened it to find Emma greeting her with a warm smile.

"Hi, Emma. Come on in," Johanna said, gesturing for Emma to come inside.

"I know I'm early," Emma said stepping over the threshold. "But I really have to pee, I'm sorry." She smiled nervously and looked around the room.

Johanna pointed to the left. "First door on the right."

Emma ran quickly down the hallway and dodged into the bathroom. Johanna and Maggie laughed at the very audible sigh of relief they heard Emma make.

Johanna wondered if she should wait for her or just carry on as normal. She went into the kitchen and took the rice off the burner. Maggie appeared behind her and placed a supportive hand on her shoulder.

"Are you good?" she whispered to Johanna.

Johanna grabbed a paper towel and wiped the sweat that dripped down her face. She took a deep breath and nodded. "I missed my dose yesterday and I was going to get caught up today, but I was so surprised by her showing up, I forgot."

"Oh crap, Jo. You're going on two days."

"I know, I know."

"Why didn't you tell me?"

"I'll be okay."

"But you're already showing the signs."

Johanna ran a glass of water and drank it down. She hung her head over the sink. "I just need a little time. It'll pass."

"Are you sure? I can tell her to leave."

"This was your idea so we're gonna do this."

Maggie sighed heavily and refilled Johanna's glass. "Here, have some more."

Johanna laughed softly and drank a little more water. She closed her eyes and took a deep breath. "You know it's too late to take it now. It's just going to have to be a rough night for me."

"I'm sorry, Jo."

"It's all right." Johanna smiled and straightened up. "It's not the first time I've forgotten to take my meds, and it surely won't be the last."

THE MISSING PIECE

Maggie smiled half-heartedly at her. She was worried. Johanna could see it.

The toilet flushed in the bathroom and the two women looked at each other. "Well," Johanna sighed. "We've been waiting a long time for this. We better just get it over with."

Emma couldn't believe she showed up and ran straight to the bathroom. They must think she's an absolute idiot. She washed her hands under the warm stream of water and dried them. She checked herself in the mirror and smiled at her reflection. She looked decent. She liked her no makeup look. Less work.

The best part about being in the small town of Bridger was that no one knew who she was. No one was staring in her face, smiling at her, and asking her asinine questions about Ericka. Here she was a normal person. She smiled at the thought.

It feels good being normal.

She was about to open the door when she noticed that the mirror was a medicine cabinet. She knew she shouldn't look but couldn't help herself. She opened it carefully and inspected the contents. There was a small first aid box, a bottle of Benadryl, and a couple of prescription medicine bottles. She glanced behind her; the coast was clear.

She picked up the first bottle and then the second. They both belonged to Johanna. She didn't recognize the name of the first one but the second one she'd seen in her research.

Methadone.

"I knew she had to be an addict," she said to herself. "To be with Nancy for so long, I knew it." She quickly read her prescription and placed it back onto the shelf.

She closed the medicine cabinet door and sighed. She felt terrible for snooping like that. It was none of her business. She checked her appearance one more time before joining them in the main room.

When Emma entered the main room, she saw them in the kitchen, huddled close together, talking. "Hi, sorry about that," she called out to them. "When you gotta go, you gotta go, right?"

The two women joined Emma in the main room. Emma felt like they could see her guilt written all over her face. It was hard for her to maintain eye contact with Johanna. Just when she started to admire her, finding out about her issues put a damper on that.

"Are you feeling okay?" Johanna asked reaching out and touching Emma gently on the arm.

"Yeah. It was long drive here from the hotel. I should've gone to the restroom before I left."

"I can understand that." Johanna guided her to the couch and sat down. "Thanks for coming to dinner."

"No problem." Emma looked around the room. It had many of the same rustic decorations that Charlotte's House had. "Something smells good. What did you cook?"

"Ribeye steaks with rice and asparagus. And lemon cake for dessert."

"Oh wow! That sounds great. Lemon cake is one of my favorites."

"Mine, too," Johanna said softly.

Maggie slipped into the spot next to Emma. "Well, you two can have that lemon cake. I hate it. Jo makes the stuff just to torture me."

Johanna laughed and clenched her hands in her lap. Emma glanced down at them and noticed the slight tremble.

"Oh well, more for us, right?" Emma addressed Johanna.

"Absolutely. Would you like something to drink?"

"What do you have?"

"We have water, lemonade, and milk."

"I'll take a glass of milk."

Johanna hopped up and hurried to the kitchen. Emma watched her walk over to the cupboard and pull a glass from it. She placed it on the counter and retrieved a jug of milk from the fridge. When she poured it, Emma saw her hands trembling so badly that she spilled a little milk.

Johanna turned in her direction and caught her watching her. She smiled and wiped up the mess. She appeared a moment later and handed the glass to Emma.

"Hey, are you alright?" Emma asked. "Why are you trembling like that?"

"Oh..." Johanna looked at Maggie and sighed. "Well, I just forgot to take my medication for today."

"What kind of medication, if you don't mind me asking?"

"No, I don't mind you asking, but how about we eat dinner before it gets too cold?" she sidestepped Emma's question and made her way back into the kitchen. She plated the food and brought it to the dining table.

"This looks great," Emma said with a smile. "Nice dodge by the way."

"Thank you," Johanna said placing the plates down. "Sit anywhere you like."

Emma chose the seat directly across from Johanna. She'd already decided that she was going to get answers tonight. Either they'd give her Jane Doe's name, or they'd provide her with her phone number. Whichever one, she didn't care, but she wasn't leaving until she had something to go on.

Maggie sat down and immediately started eating. Emma watched her with amusement. She ate fast, amazingly fast. Maggie paused to take a sip of lemonade. She looked over at Emma and frowned.

"What?" she asked.

"Nothing," Emma laughed. "I've never seen anyone eat so fast in my life."

Johanna chuckled and slid a forkful of rice into her mouth. "I'm sure she could set a world record."

"Oh, you're so funny," Maggie said, rolling her eyes. She ignored them and finished off the rest of her meal in one minute.

Emma counted.

After they'd finished teasing Maggie, Johanna and Emma ate in silence. Emma had planned on asking a series of probing questions during dinner, but something about Johanna made her refrain from doing so. In her home environment, Johanna seemed more guarded, less relaxed. Emma knew that if she started in on her with a bunch of questions, Johanna would get offended and kick her out. So, she waited until the right time.

The right time came after dinner when they retreated to the living room and watched the fire burn in the fireplace. Everything about Johanna's home was inviting and warm. Even though she wanted to grill them both about her mother, she couldn't bring herself to do it. She couldn't explain the peace that she felt when she was there with them. It was something that she never experienced before.

Johanna and Maggie chit chatted about work and something about an upcoming arts festival at Jackson Hole.

"Arts festival?" Emma asked. She loved all forms of art, but she never really had a chance to fully explore them. Ericka wanted her in the corporate sector, so anything creative was discouraged.

"Yes. The annual fall arts festival is coming up in a week. We've been preparing the ladies to enter some of their arts for judging," Johanna said.

"Oh, that's cool. What kind of arts?"

Johanna picked up her tablet. "I'll show you." She motioned for Emma to scoot closer. When Emma came closer, Johanna scrolled through her gallery. "We have many talented women at Charlotte's House. Every year we have at least one resident who places in the competitions."

Emma smiled. "All of it is beautiful. You're right. They're definitely talented."

"They have an awesome instructor," Maggie chimed in.

"Oh really?" Emma asked. "Who?" Maggie pointed to Johanna and winked. Emma's mouth dropped open. There were so many layers of this woman that it amazed her.

"It's not that impressive. It's therapeutic. And someone has to do it," Johanna said with a smile.

"You must know your art if you can teach different mediums like that. I love all forms of art. Music, painting, drawing, poetry, but my adoptive mother didn't like my creative side. She wanted me to follow in her footsteps and stroke the egos of rich executives."

"Oh, that's interesting."

"Yeah, I guess."

"Which form of art is your favorite?"

Emma considered the question for a moment. "I like painting with oil."

"Me, too," Johanna stated.

"I like the fact that once the paint goes on, it's like a forever thing. It's as if the artist's vision is forever etched on the canvas, all the way down to the fibers of it. It's like they become one, the artist and the canvas." She took the tablet from Johanna's hand and scrolled through the rest of the photo gallery.

"I'm working on an oil painting now," Johanna said.

"Really? Of what?"

"There's an overlook point west of here called Eagle's Ridge. I like to relax and read there. I'm painting it so I'll always have it with me."

"May I see it?"

"Um," Johanna hesitated. "Sure, why not." She motioned for Emma to follow her up the stairs to her level of the house. There was a room off to the left that had a tall beautiful window. "This way."

Johanna turned on the light revealing a simple art studio with an easel and large canvas positioned in the middle of the room in front of the window.

Emma went straight to the easel, her eyes immediately drawn to the landscape painting sitting on it. It looked so real it seemed like she was looking out of a window. She'd never been to this place, but Johanna painted it so perfectly life-like that she didn't have to travel there to know what it looked like.

"Wow, this is beautiful," she whispered. She wanted to reach out and touch it, but the paint looked wet. "Are you finished with it?"

"Almost," Johanna said sitting down on the stool in front of the canvas. "I can be a perfectionist at times. It feels like there's something missing from it."

"What's missing?"

Johanna shrugged and stared at the painting. "I'm not sure." She sat quietly for a few minutes, just staring at the painting. "It'll come to me one day."

Emma gazed at the canvas and smiled. "I can't believe how real that looks. You did that from memory?"

"Yes."

"Could you take me there?" Emma blurted out.

Johanna nodded slowly. "When would you like to go?"

Emma glanced back at the painting. "Whenever it looks like this. That's when I want to go."

Johanna chuckled. "You're in luck. It looks like this all day except at sunset. Then the western sky is deep with reds, oranges, and purples."

"That's great. Can we go tomorrow?" Emma asked.

"Sure."

"Maybe you can call Jane Doe and ask her to meet us out there. That'll be nice. Kill two birds with one stone."

When Johanna's smile faded away Emma knew she'd said the wrong thing. But she wasn't there to make friends. She was there to find her mother.

"I see," Johanna said stepping away from her. She walked over to the doorway and switched off the light.

Emma hurried to join her. Johanna shut the door behind them and guided Emma over to the sitting area.

"I don't have to be at work until twelve tomorrow. We can go to Eagle's Ridge in the morning," she said motioning toward the couch. "It'll be better if you stay the night so we can get there early."

"Stay the night?"

"Yes. Unless you have an objection."

"No, no," Emma said. "It just seemed like you were pissed just now."

Johanna laughed and sat down beside her. "I have nothing to be upset about, Emma. I know why you're here and I'd like to help you get acquainted with your mother, but this is a very delicate situation."

"Delicate how?"

Johanna sighed and wrung her hands. "I don't want you to be disappointed."

"Disappointed how?"

"Disappointed in her," Johanna said softly. "And in who she is."

"What do you mean?" Emma noticed a bead of sweat dripping from Johanna's face. Johanna reached up and swiped it away quickly.

"She's not anything like your adoptive parents, sweetheart. She doesn't have anything to offer you. She doesn't have much to her name. She's a nobody."

Emma frowned. "What? I don't care if she doesn't have anything and I hope she's not like my adoptive parents." Emma's heart twisted inside of her chest. "My adoptive parents loved me with their money and not their affection, so I hope to God she's not like them."

Johanna sighed and looked down at her hands. "You're probably used to having whatever you want, whenever you want it. You've got to understand that your mother doesn't have the means to do any of that."

"Any of what? What are you talking about?"

"Never mind," Johanna said. "I'm not making much sense, I'm sorry."

"Listen," Emma scooted closer to her. "It's obvious that you know her better than you let on earlier, so you might as well tell me."

"Tell you what?"

"Tell me what you're hiding. Tell me why everyone around her is protecting her."

"Because she wanted the events surrounding your birth to be kept secret," Johanna answered quickly.

"Why? Was she a victim of a sexual assault or something?"

"No."

"Was she sleeping with the President?"

Johanna laughed. "No, of course not."

"Then what's the big deal?"

"It's because of her family."

Emma nodded. Now she was getting somewhere. "What about her family?"

"She'd already disgraced them so much when she started using. There were times when she'd be so high that she'd walk down Main Street bare naked, exposing herself to the whole world. People talked about the family so badly."

"Did they try to help her? Her family, I mean."

Johanna nibbled on her fingernail. "Yes. Everyone tried, especially her family, but once she started using the heavier drugs, they cut her off and it was harder to get through to her."

"Heavier drugs? How did that all start?"

Johanna leaned back into the corner of the couch. "Are you sure you want to know all of this?"

"The more I know, the better prepared I'll be when I meet her."

Johanna stared at her for a few long moments before finally nodding in agreement.

"Before she became an addict, she lived a pretty decent life. She was a model citizen if you will. During one of our annual events, she was thrown from her horse and injured. She got away with several broken ribs and a broken collarbone. She was lucky she didn't break her neck."

"Oh man."

"The doctors prescribed her some pretty strong painkillers to help her manage through the pain. They gave her morphine and hydrocodone."

"I've read about those."

"Yeah, well long story short, she got hooked on the pain killers. She had a boyfriend who was a good man, but he enabled her."

"How?"

"Even though he knew she was hooked, he'd get her the meds whenever she ran out. She'd act like a jerk with him until he gave in and got her some. Classic drug dependency behavior." Her voice trailed off as she gazed into Emma's eyes. Although she was looking directly at her, Johanna seemed to be a million miles away.

"That's sad."

"Sure was. Well this continued for several years. She was able to hide her addiction from the family, but one day they found out. They were more concerned with how her addiction would make them look than how to help her."

"What did they do?"

"They covered up the problem and tried to help her their own way. Eventually, she started craving something stronger. That's when she started doing heroin and that's when she started getting in trouble with the law."

"What kind of trouble?"

"Bouncing checks, shoplifting, prostituting herself in exchange for drugs."

"Oh man..." Emma felt a wave of nausea wash over her. It was then that she realized she ate her entire meal at dinnertime and didn't vomit once. That's progress.

"Yes, definitely not the kind of person you'd want to be friends with."

"Is that how she ended up at Redemption Valley?"

"Yes. Nance went to the same church as her parents, so they reached out to her for help. She vowed to take care of her while she was there in her care."

"That's what Nancy must've meant when she said that she was responsible for her."

"Yes. She was her guardian angel." Johanna sighed deeply. Her body language gave off all kinds of signs that she was uncomfortable. "Anyway, she was in and out of Redemption, struggling hard to maintain her sobriety, but it was hard for her."

"Why was it so hard?"

THE MISSING PIECE

"The only people she had were the people at Redemption. Nance, Mags, and the others. Outside, her family had disowned her until she cleaned up, so she didn't have the support she needed. She easily slipped back into the habit."

Emma took a minute to process everything that Johanna had said. It was a lot more than she'd expected, but it was a great start. Johanna seemed to know personal details that only someone close to Jane Doe would know.

"Nancy said that the last time she was released she got pregnant with me while she was out. Do you know anything about that?"

Johanna leaned back and stared at the ceiling. "She didn't even know she was pregnant with you."

"So, I guess there's no possibility she knew who my father was, huh?"

"Honestly, your father is an unknown person. He could have been anyone, but most likely a guy just passing through."

Emma wasn't sure what it was, but the way Johanna said that hit her extremely hard. She came to the realization that she was just a mistake. A chance happening between a woman who was high on drugs and a man who wanted her.

"Well... That's comforting," she said with a laugh.

Johanna glanced over at her. "I'm sorry. I shouldn't have broken it to you like that. I wish I could tell you they were high school sweethearts with a fairy tale relationship, but I can't."

"I get it," Emma said quietly. "It just sucks to hear it."

Johanna sat up and stretched. "I'm going to turn in for the night. We'll leave around five so get your rest."

"Five in the morning?"

"Yes."

"Wonderful."

Johanna got up and disappeared into her dark room. She reappeared a few minutes later with a pillow and a blanket. "The couch folds out."

"Thanks."

"If you need anything, just let either me or Mags know."

"Will do."

"We'll talk more tomorrow."

"Are you going to invite Jane Doe along as well?"

"Is that what you really want?"

"Yes. It is."

Johanna nodded. "All right then. Goodnight."

"Good night."

Emma watched Johanna disappear into that room again and shut the door behind her. A light came on underneath the door and she saw her shadow moving back and forth in the room. It seemed like she was pacing.

"Why is she so nervous?" Emma asked herself.

From where she was sitting, she could see Maggie sitting on the couch watching tv. Maggie was helpful with the information she shared, and Johanna outpoured so much information that Emma needed a few hours to process it. These two knew her mother better than anyone, it seemed.

Emma moved the coffee table out of the way and pulled the bed from the couch. She made the bed with the linens Johanna had given her and climbed in. It was cozier than most sofa beds that she'd slept on in the past, but definitely not the most comfortable.

She exhaled a deep breath and stared at the same ceiling that Johanna was staring at earlier. She smiled, feeling like she knew her mother a little bit more now than she did when she arrived. Johanna had given her so much information. She'd given it freely. She didn't have to force it out of her, it just flowed.

She closed her eyes and let the events of the day replay in her mind. If all goes well, she'll be meeting her mother tomorrow. She was scared and excited both at the same time. She'd waited years for this, and it was finally going to happen.

11

Emma awakened to the smell of bacon frying. It was her most favorite smell in the entire universe, making a smile instantly cross her face. She rolled over and faced the direction of the balcony. She heard the voices of Johanna and Maggie from downstairs. They chatted about work and the arts festival. She heard Maggie ask Johanna if she'd taken her medicine yet. Emma found it odd that only after a few minutes of eavesdropping that neither of the women mentioned anything about Jane Doe.

When she heard Johanna walking up the stairs, she pulled the covers over her head and pretended to be sleeping. Johanna walked over to Emma's side of the bed and stood quietly. Emma felt her presence. She was watching her. Emma turned over, pretending like she was just waking up. She opened her eyes and was greeted with a warm smile.

"You have twenty minutes to clean up and eat before we leave," Johanna said, placing a towel and washcloth on the coffee table.

Emma sat up. "Twenty minutes? That's all?"

"I've been up for a couple of hours. You seemed like you needed the rest."

Emma stretched and yawned. "Man, I guess I did. Thanks."

"No problem."

"Something smells good," Emma said with a smile.

"I made bacon and eggs."

"Yum."

"There's plenty left," Johanna said as she sat down in the recliner adjacent from the couch. She rolled her neck, popping it loudly before glancing down at her watch. "Fifteen minutes."

"There's no way it's been five minutes already."

Johanna shrugged and grabbed the television remote, switching it to CNN for the morning news. She ignored Emma's remark and focused on the news report.

Emma groaned. She hated being rushed but she was at the mercy of this woman today. Johanna was going to reunite her with her mother. Emma was beyond excited. When she reached for her phone on the side table, she felt warm liquid rush into her underwear. She threw back the covers and crawled out of bed.

"Where's the bathroom?" she asked. Her voice was on the edge of panic.

Johanna pointed down the hallway. "Straight ahead at the end of the hallway." She noticed the panicked expression on Emma's face and got up out of her seat. "What is it?" she asked.

Emma glanced back at the sofa bed. "I'm sorry, I think I might've—" Embarrassment had choked the words right out of her mouth.

Johanna followed her gaze, her eyes settling on the crimson stain where Emma had been sitting. She rushed to Emma's side, but Emma backed away from her and sprinted into the bathroom.

Emma closed the door behind her and walked over to the mirror. She leaned against the sink. Her body trembled as she stared at her reflection in the mirror. She felt it again. The familiar warmth flowing out of her.

"Oh no," she whispered to herself. "This can't be happening."

She maneuvered herself to the toilet and sat down. As the minutes rolled by, she couldn't move, she couldn't think. All she could do was stare at her blood-stained underwear and wonder how this could be happening to her. Why now?

There was a knock at the door. Through the fog in her mind, Emma heard the soft voice of Johanna calling her from the other side.

"Emma, are you okay?"

Emma wanted to stay hidden, away from the eyes of anyone who'd judge her. She should've gone to the

THE MISSING PIECE

doctor while she was still in Chicago. Maybe she shouldn't have taken that long drive. Maybe it was too much.

"Please go away," Emma said.

Johanna knocked firmer. "Open the door. Do you need help?"

"I don't know."

"Emma, please."

Eventually Emma got up and answered the door. When she cracked it open, all she saw was Johanna's concerned face.

"What's wrong?" Johanna asked.

Emma felt a lump rise into her throat. "I don't know. I'm bleeding."

"Are you in pain?"

"No. I mean, just a little cramping."

"How far along are you?"

Emma shrugged. "I don't know exactly, but at least a month maybe. When I took the test, I'd just missed my period."

"You haven't been to the doctor yet?"

"No," Emma said lowering her head.

"We need to get you to a doctor."

As much as Emma wanted to protest, she knew Johanna was right. "Okay. I'll go. But I need to shower first."

Johanna patted her on the shoulder. "I'll go get you a fresh change of clothes. I'll be right back," she said disappearing out of the room.

Emma turned on the shower and stripped out of her clothes. She crawled into the shower and sat under the water stream. She didn't want to think of what could be happening. All she wanted to do was shower. When Cal's face flashed into her mind, she was overwhelmed with sadness. He didn't want the child they had made together. He couldn't possibly get his way after breaking her heart like he did.

She didn't know how long she'd been sitting in the shower before she finally decided to get out. Johanna had left a change of clothing folded neatly on the sink countertop. Emma dressed in silence, looking at herself one last time before leaving the bathroom.

When she came out, Johanna and Maggie were waiting for her. They both had looks of intense concern on their faces. Emma held back her tears, but her cramps had started to intensify slightly. The pain was mostly in her back. Maybe it was the implantation bleeding that she'd read about online. Maybe that was it.

She was overwhelmed in her heart with the what-ifs. Johanna slipped her arm around her waist and helped her walk downstairs. The entire way to the car, Johanna spoke softly to her in her ear, but she couldn't hear her voice through the panicked thoughts racing in her mind. Maggie was waiting at the car holding the door open for them when they got there. She helped Johanna put Emma into the car and closed the door behind her.

Johanna rushed around the car and hopped into the driver's seat then sped away to the hospital. Emma felt like she was stuck in an endless loop of a dream sequence she couldn't escape.

12

Johanna checked her watch again. It'd been nearly forty-five minutes since the doctor went in to see Emma. He'd come out once and called in a nurse who was carrying a tray of empty specimen vials. When she heard footsteps approaching, she turned to see Nancy coming down the hallway.

Johanna smiled when she sat down next to her. "Hey," she greeted Nancy.

"How is she?"

"I'm not sure," Johanna said with a sigh. "They've been in there for a while."

"Mags told me what happened."

Johanna nodded. "I hope it's nothing serious."

"Did you tell her yet?" Nancy asked. When Johanna didn't respond, Nancy placed a hand on her shoulder. "Jo, did you tell her?"

"No, I haven't had a chance to."

"Why not?"

"The timing hasn't been right. I was going to tell her when I took her to Eagle's Ridge this morning, but this happened."

"Jo," Nancy said taking her hand. "If she's lost her baby, she's going to need you."

"I don't know how to do that."

"How to do what?"

"Be what she needs," she said in a hushed whisper. "Look at me!"

"I see you and what I see is a kind, generous, and loving person. You're exactly what she needs right now."

"I'm a mess." Johanna wrung her hands nervously. "She deserves better than me."

"What she deserves is to know that she's found you. Don't let her go home empty handed."

Tears stung the backs of Johanna's eyes. She swallowed the lump in her throat. "She's going to be disappointed that it's me."

"Why don't you let her decide that? Right now, she needs someone to be here for her. She's alone and away from her family."

"I know."

The door to Emma's room swung open and the doctor came out walking towards them. Nancy greeted him first.

"Hi Tom, how is she?" she asked, giving him a quick side hug.

"She took the news okay. The urine test we gave her came back negative for pregnancy. From our calculations, Miss Benson was about six and a half weeks pregnant. We performed an ultrasound and no fetal heartbeat was detected."

"Oh, dear God. How sad." Nancy gasped.

"The whole process should just take a few more hours since her body is expelling larger amounts of pregnancy tissue now."

Johanna's stomach twisted into knots. She squeezed her eyes shut, trying to force the images of Emma's inevitable heartbreak out of her mind.

"Can we see her?" Johanna asked.

"Yes. We're admitting her for the night to keep an eye on her." He touched Nancy lightly on the shoulder. "If you need anything, just ring one of the nurses."

"Thanks, Tom," Nancy said. "Tell your wife I said hi."

The doctor nodded his head and walked away, leaving Johanna and Nancy standing there, stunned.

Johanna slumped down into her chair and sighed heavily. Nancy sat down next to her and put her arm around her.

"I'm sorry, Jo," she said softly.

"I don't understand why all of this is happening now."

"I stopped questioning things like this a long time ago." Nancy pulled her in closer and sighed. "But now's not the time to ask why these things are happening. Now's the time to act."

"Act? What difference will I make?"

"You'll make a big difference if you just go in there and be with her."

"I plan to be there for her, but nothing I say or do will make what's happened any better for her. How can I possibly make her feel better?"

"Perhaps it's not meant for you to make her feel better right now. Maybe all you need to do is be there."

Johanna groaned and rubbed her hands over her face. She was shaking now, more than usual. "I don't know what to say."

"Nothing really needs to be said, Jo. She's alone in a town with no friends. Just be there."

Johanna wiped a tear from her face. "Yeah."

"It wasn't a coincidence that this happened to her right after she showed up in town."

Johanna sniffled. "What are you talking about?"

"She's exactly where she needs to be. She's home."

Nancy's words landed heavily on her heart. Johanna laid her head on Nancy's shoulder and stared at the door to Emma's room. She knew Nancy was right. After a few minutes of quiet reflection, Johanna decided to go and sit with Emma.

Emma turned over in the bed and hugged her pillow. She was numb. She wanted to go to sleep and not wake up for a while. Cal had gotten his wish. That bastard. Of all the people that she'd ever met he was the one she'd misjudged the most. She thought he was the one for her. Although it scared her to death, she was willing to give it a try. But not him. It was his way or no way.

She remembered the pain she felt when he made her choose between him and the baby. What was she supposed to do? And now... What is she supposed to do now? Go back to him?

When the door opened slowly, Emma looked up to see Johanna step in. She watched her enter and close the door behind her. Johanna said nothing as she approached Emma's bed and pulled up a chair. She sat down, never once taking her eyes off of Emma.

"Hey there," Johanna said with a disarming smile.

"I was about to go to sleep." Emma didn't want to be rude to her. She just wanted to be alone. She couldn't let her see her cry. "Can you come back later?"

"If you don't mind, I'd like to stay."

"Why?"

"Because I'd like to make sure you're okay."

"I'm fine."

Johanna sighed and scooted closer. She smiled again and cleared her throat. "I spoke to the doctor."

"And?" Emma's front was crumbling, her lip trembled as she struggled to hold back her tears. She held Johanna's gaze for as long as she could. Her vision blurred as the tears finally forced their way out. She blinked them out of her eyes.

"I am so sorry, Emma." Johanna said, taking Emma's hand and squeezing it. "I wish there was something I could say to make it better."

"There's nothing to say. Nothing to do."

"Do you need me to call someone?" Johanna asked.

"No," she answered quickly. "No one cares, trust me."

"No one?"

Emma released Johanna's hand and turned over onto her back. Her stomach cramped more now. She gripped her belly and cringed because of the pain.

"I texted my mom when I was on the way here. She read my message but never responded."

"Did you tell her what happened?"

Emma laughed. "Yeah right. She doesn't even know I was pregnant."

"I see. What about your boyfriend?"

Emma stared at the ceiling. "Oh him? He dumped me when I told him about the baby."

"I'm sorry, I didn't know."

"That's okay. I have my BFF, but I can't talk to her right now. I'll lose it."

"I understand."

Emma sniffled and kept staring at the ceiling. Her mind replayed the months of happiness she had with Cal. How could she have been so wrong? Everything that they did together made her feel like he wanted to be with her.

He told her that he loved her. Numerous times. He was always the first to say it.

"Are you all right?" Johanna's voice cut through the chaos of her thoughts.

"I guess." But she really wasn't. She was falling apart from the inside out. Nothing had gone her way. She thought by now she would be hanging out with her mother, enjoying her company and talking about their lives, but instead, she was confined to a hospital bed, feeling the life of her child drain out of her body.

Her phone rang, startling her. She answered it quickly. "Mom?"

"Hello, Emma."

"Mom…" Emma choked up at the sound of Ericka's voice. "How are you?"

THE MISSING PIECE

"I'm a little busy today. How are you?" As usual Ericka's voice was cold and disinterested. "Are you calling for money?"

"No." Emma swallowed the lump in her throat. "I'm in the hospital."

"Hospital? What's happened?"

"I need to tell you something, Mom."

"Well, go on and say it."

Emma squeezed the tears out of her eyes and sighed deeply. She'd forgotten that Johanna was in the room with her until she looked over and saw her reassuring face. "I'm in the hospital because I'm having a miscarriage."

"A what?" Ericka gasped.

"I was pregnant, and I was going to tell you and Dad when I got back home."

Ericka went silent on the other end. All Emma could hear was the sound of her heavy angry breaths.

"Please say something, Mom."

Ericka uttered something indecipherable and laughed. "Why am I not surprised?"

"I'm sorry, Mom. Don't be angry with me, please."

"You've never made good choices for yourself and this is just more proof. It's that O'Brannigan boy's baby, isn't it?"

"Yes. It was. But Cal broke up with me."

"He broke up with you. Why?"

"He didn't want a baby. He wanted me to choose between him and the baby."

"Good for him. You see, Emma. This is exactly what I'm talking about. You make these rash decisions and you don't care how your decisions effect other people."

"Mom, please." Emma knew it was a bad idea to tell her, but she hoped that just maybe Ericka would feel a little sympathy for her. "I'm going through a lot right now."

"Well, I'm sorry to hear you're going through some things, but don't come home until you sort those things out. I don't need anyone getting wind of this new stunt of yours and having this spread all over social media."

Emma glanced over at Johanna and realized that she could hear every word that Ericka was saying. Johanna looked angry.

"I would like to come home after I get released from the hospital."

"You heard what I said Emma."

"No one will find out."

"Stay where you are until you work this out. Then come home. I don't need the negative press right before the fall gala."

Another rejection... "Fine. I'll stay away for a while." Emma held the phone and listened to Ericka's silent reproach. Although she wasn't saying anything, Emma could almost hear Ericka's thoughts.

"I need to go," Ericka said sharply. "I'll tell your father to transfer some money if you need it."

"I don't need any money, but thanks." Emma was on the verge of tears. "Bye, Mom." She quickly disconnected the phone and held it against her chest. She felt like her chest was going to explode.

After a while, she placed the phone down on the table next to her bed and relaxed on the pillow. She couldn't bring herself to look at Johanna. She was too embarrassed. No one had ever heard Ericka speak so harshly to Emma before. This was an uncomfortable first.

"I'm sorry you had to hear that."

"I'm sorry you had to endure it." Johanna's voice was comforting. It made Emma feel like everything would be okay.

Emma grabbed her stomach and curled up into a ball. She was gripped by another round of cramps, even stronger than the last. She clenched the bed railing, her hand trembled as she held on tightly to it. She told herself she wasn't going to cry about the pain because it just felt like a really bad period, but as she thought about Cal's rejection, and then her inability to find her mother, and then Ericka's stinging reproach, her heart couldn't take anymore.

A sound came out of her mouth that she didn't even recognize. Her emotional pain was far greater than her physical pain. She'd never felt pain like this before in her life. It was unreal. Cal and Ericka's words bounced off each other in her head. She wanted nothing more than to clear them out, but they kept getting louder and louder. But then over the sound of their voices in her head, she heard her own sobs increasing in volume.

She felt Johanna's hand cover her hand that was gripping the side of the bed. She opened her eyes to see Johanna watching her. Johanna's eyes were filled with tears. Her lips moved, but Emma couldn't hear her voice. She could read her lips though. Johanna kept saying the same thing over and over again.

She said. "I'm here."

13

A few days had passed since Emma's miscarriage when she finally decided to get out of bed and visit with Johanna and Maggie. Lexie called nearly every day, several times a day, but she didn't feel like talking. She finally had to have the much-dreaded conversation with her. She told Lexie about everything, including Ericka's telling her to stay away until she got her issues sorted out. She let her know that she'd be away longer than she'd originally planned and asked her not to worry. Lexie respected her wish for distance and privacy and backed off.

Emma heard Maggie and Johanna talking in the kitchen below. She decided that she was going to get up and act like a normal human being and maybe she'd get the honor of meeting her mother. She assumed that they told her what had happened which is why she hadn't shown up yet.

She got dressed and went downstairs. Their conversation came to an abrupt end when she entered the room. Maggie sipped her coffee and Johanna scrolled through her iPad.

"Good morning," Emma greeted them.

"Good morning," Johanna said getting up from her seat and walking over to her. She put her arm around Emma and squeezed gently. "How are you feeling?"

"Thankful that you gave me a place to stay for a few days. The hotel wasn't as comfy as this place."

"It's my pleasure." She pointed to the seat next to Maggie. "Are you hungry?"

"Yes, actually I'm starving."

Johanna chuckled. "I'm not surprised. You haven't eaten anything substantial in a few days."

"Has it been that long?"

Johanna nodded. "Mags made breakfast. I hope you like it," she said placing a plate down in front of Emma.

"What is it?" Emma said, eyeing the plate suspiciously.

"A spinach and mushroom quiche," Maggie answered.

"For breakfast?" Emma scrunched up her nose.

"Don't knock it till you try it, kid." Maggie winked at her and got up from her seat. "I'm outta here. See you later."

Johanna waved goodbye and watched her leave. When Maggie drove off, she turned back to Emma. "So, how are you really?"

Emma shrugged. "Better, I guess."

"Do you feel like getting out of the house today?"

"I don't know."

"It'll do you some good, I promise."

Emma cut a piece of the quiche and slid it into her mouth. She frowned, chewing slowly. "Oh my God. This is so gross."

Johanna laughed.

"Don't tell her I said that," Emma said with a smile.

"You've got nothing to worry about there. I dare not tell her."

Their laughter eventually turned into an uncomfortable silence. Johanna cleared her throat and sighed. "I took the day off to do some errands. Would you like to tag along?"

Emma considered her offer for a moment. "What's in it for me?"

Johanna shrugged. "I could take you to Eagle's Ridge if you'd like. It's beautiful around this time."

Emma focused on the quiche on her plate again. She stabbed at it, cutting it into tiny bite-sized pieces. "I don't think I'd be good company for you today."

"Come on, it'll be fun."

Emma sighed and sat back in her seat. It was obvious that Johanna wasn't going to take no for an answer. "Can I ask you something?"

"Yes. You can ask me anything."

"Would you be offended if I left?"

"Left? As in went back to the hotel?"

"No. Leave as in leave town."

Johanna swallowed hard. "Why would you leave now?"

Emma laughed a little. "I'm surprised you'd even ask that question. You know I came here looking for my mother and it's pretty obvious that she doesn't want to meet me. She knows I'm here. She probably even knows what happened to me, but she never showed. It's obvious to me that she doesn't want to see me."

"Emma, listen—"

"No," she interrupted. "Don't tell me that she cares for me or wants to see me, because I know it's not true. Plus, I just think I've used up enough of your kindness and time already."

Johanna sighed and toyed with her fingers. "If you must go then first come with me to Eagle's Ridge."

"What's so important about it?"

"It's just a special place and I want to share it with you."

Johanna's statement landed awkwardly on Emma's heart. All Emma wanted to do was disappear from everyone, but Johanna was inviting her to spend some time with her on her day off.

"You want to share a place that's special to you with me?"

"Yes. I do."

"Why?"

"Because I want to show you that the world is a lot bigger than where you come from."

"What do you mean by that?"

"I just mean that sometimes it's easy to get so wrapped up in the people and things around us that we forget that there's another world out there. And there's so much beauty to it."

Emma said nothing.

"Let me show you my world before you go back to yours."

Emma couldn't understand what was happening, but the offer was intriguing. What kind of a person would she be if she rejected Johanna's offer after she'd taken care of her for so many days?

"Your world, huh?"

"Yes."

"What does your world include?"

"Well let's see. Horses, mountains, rivers, birds, and hiking trails, just to name a few."

Emma nodded. "All of that sounds nice."

"So, what do you say? Would you like to tag along?"

Emma thought it over for a while. The sooner she gave Johanna what she wanted, the sooner she could leave town and never look back. Perhaps even start over someplace where no one knew who she was.

"Sure," she said. "I'll go with you, but after we're done, I'm leaving, okay?"

Johanna nodded. "That's fair."

"Do I need to wear anything special like gear or something?"

"Gear?"

"Yeah. I'm assuming you want to take me hiking."

"Just wear long pants, sturdy shoes and long sleeves. I'll have everything else."

"So, we are going hiking."

"I didn't say that. You just assumed."

"Well whatever we do, I hope it's not too strenuous because I'm not back to one hundred percent yet and I want to rest enough before I drive back."

"Relax. It won't be too much." She patted Emma's hand. "I plan to leave in a half hour."

Emma smiled. "I'll be ready."

Johanna stopped at the diner so Emma could eat breakfast. They took a seat in the corner by the window and ordered off the menu. Johanna ordered a cup of decaf and Emma ordered a bacon and eggs breakfast plate.

"That's the most popular item on the menu," Johanna said taking her jacket off and placing it beside her in the booth.

This was the first time that Emma noticed Johanna's tattoo. At first glance, she certainly didn't seem like the type to have any. On her inner forearm was a beautiful work of art. It was some type of flower that had been etched with fine detail. It almost looked real. Underneath it was a name—Mila.

"What? Haven't you ever seen a tattoo before?" Johanna asked.

Emma laughed softly. "Of course, I have, you just don't seem like the type."

"Oh? Why not?"

"You seem so put together."

"I'm everything but that."

"What kind of flower is that?" Emma reached for Johanna's arm, turning it over and inspecting it further.

"It's a magnolia."

"This artwork is amazing! There's so much detail that it looks real. How long did it take the artist to do this?"

"About four or five hours."

"That must've been painful."

"I've experienced worse," Johanna pulled back her arm and folded it against her chest. "The pain was temporary, but worth it." Johanna glanced over Emma's shoulder. Victoria, the waitress, approached with their orders and placed them on the table.

"Oh, that looks good!" Emma said.

"It sure does," Johanna added.

"It's the best dish on the menu, I guarantee it," Victoria said. She slid the check to Johanna. "There you go, Jo."

"Thanks, Vicks. How long are you working today?"

"Till four. Then me and the boys are heading up to the Ridge and hitting the trail for a couple of hours." Victoria leaned against the booth seat and wiped the sweat from her brow. "There're not many good days left before the cold weather rolls in."

"I know. We're headed up there later."

"That's cool. If you run across our camp, stop in and stay a while. I'm making my famous mint cocoa tonight."

"Yum, sounds good. Where're you guys setting up camp?"

"Near Zander's Pass."

"All right. We'll stop in for a while if we make it there."

"Great. Talk to you later, Jo." She turned to Emma and smiled. "And I hope you enjoy your meal." She disappeared into the kitchen leaving the two of them sitting at the table.

Johanna stirred her coffee as she gazed out the window. Emma had already been working on her breakfast while the two women chatted. She didn't realize how hungry she was until she started eating.

"So..." Emma said taking a sip of orange juice. "Who's Mila?"

Emma waited for an answer, but she never got one. Johanna just stared out the window, her eyes were fixed on something outside. Emma followed her gaze, but she couldn't see anything but a mountain range in the distance.

"Who's Mila?" she repeated.

Johanna pulled her arms in and hugged herself. She ignored Emma's question and kept looking out the window. Emma knew what that meant. She'd crossed a boundary and Johanna wasn't going to give her any more details. And that was fine.

"I'm sorry, that's none of my business."

Johanna nodded and eventually turned her attention back to her. Emma was surprised to see tears in her eyes. Whoever Mila was, the memory of her obviously caused Johanna a great deal of pain.

"That's okay. Listen, I'm going to go use the bathroom. I'll be ready to go when I get out, so finish up, okay?"

"Yes. Okay." Emma watched her walk into the back of the diner and disappear into the bathroom. She finished off the rest of her breakfast and waited for her to return.

Johanna's reaction piqued her curiosity. She was a mysterious person, quiet and reserved, but there was a part of her that she hadn't revealed yet.

Emma thought back to how the others acted around Johanna. She was highly respected and loved. The women at Charlotte's House seemed to worship the ground she walked on, Nancy treated her like family, and she and Maggie were practically best friends. Everybody loved her.

And Emma could see why. The more time she spent with Johanna, the more her respect for her deepened. She was so caring. And gentle in all her ways. Emma wished Ericka was more like Johanna.

The front door swung open and Emma saw the Deputy Sheriff come in. He removed his sunglasses and surveyed the room. He caught sight of her almost immediately. He smiled, nodding his head at her before taking a seat at the counter.

She smiled back and avoided his gaze by pretending to be preoccupied with something on her phone. He laughed and waved Victoria over to him. Victoria came over and leaned over the counter. She whispered something to him, and they shared a laugh together. She left him briefly and returned with a cup of coffee.

Emma's heart dropped when he got up and approached her table. She looked from the right and to the left, looking for a quick means of escape, but it was no use. He had his sights on her and she couldn't get out of this encounter. Seconds later, he was waiting patiently for her to acknowledge him.

"Good morning, Deputy," Emma said politely.

"Good morning, Miss Benson. May I sit for a minute?"

"Sure, but we're going to be leaving as soon as she gets back."

He sipped his coffee. "That's no problem. Who is 'she?'"

"Johanna."

"Of course. You're in good company with Jo."

She nodded, glancing over his shoulder to see if she was coming back yet. "How can I help you, Deputy?"

"I'm just saying hello. And I—" he tugged at his necktie and straightened up in his seat. "I just wanted to say that I'm sorry to hear about your loss," he whispered.

Emma was at a loss for words. She felt exposed, like everyone knew her business. Johanna appeared at the table. She took in the scene quietly perhaps wondering what she just walked into.

"How did you know?"

"I was at the hospital when you were admitted. I asked the doctor."

"Oh." Her eyes fell away from his. She didn't expect to be reminded of her loss so soon. All she wanted to do was go back and crawl in the bed.

Johanna cleared her throat and touched him lightly on the shoulder. "Hi Paul."

"Hey, Jo," he said rising. "I was just leaving." He got up and gave Johanna a quick hug. "How're you today?"

"I'm good, thanks."

"I'm off at two. You wanna come by the ranch? I'm throwing some steaks on the grill."

"Next time, I promise. Emma and I are doing some running around and then heading up to the Ridge."

He nodded. "Okay. If you change your mind, you know where to find me."

"All right," Johanna said as she grazed her hand up his bicep. "I'll text you if I decide to come by."

He adjusted his uniform and slipped on his hat. "I'll see you two around." He turned back and looked at Emma one last time before leaving the diner.

Johanna sat down in his spot and watched Emma for a moment. "What's wrong?"

THE MISSING PIECE

Emma watched the Deputy walk to his car and get in. She shook her head slowly. "I just feel like everyone knows what happened to me. He offered his condolences."

"I'm sorry, Emma. Bridger is a small town. He meant well."

"I know. It just sucks to think everyone knows my business. That's what I hate about Chicago."

"I understand and I assure you not everyone knows what happened."

"Okay," Emma said gathering her things. "Are you ready to go, because I am." She didn't want to talk about the Deputy nor the possibility of more people knowing about her very private loss.

"Yes, I'm ready. Let's get out of here." She gestured for Emma to join her and they walked outside and hopped into Johanna's Jeep.

Emma sat quietly in the passenger's seat watching Johanna text on her phone. She was having an intense conversation with someone. Emma noticed how her cheekbones lit up with color. She looked upset.

"Is everything okay?" Emma asked.

Johanna looked over and smile. "Yes. Just finishing up conversation before we hit the road, I'm sorry. I won't be much longer."

Emma waited a little while longer. Eventually Johanna attached her phone to the dash cradle and started the Jeep. She sat there gripping the steering wheel.

"Johanna?"

"Yeah?" she said without turning towards her.

"I hate to bring this up again and I know I said that I didn't care but—"

"But you want to see your mother, right?" she said softly.

Emma nodded. "More than anything."

Johanna tightened her grip on the steering wheel. "Before this day is over, you'll see her, I promise."

"Really?"

"Yes," she whispered. "I want that more than anything too."

Emma pulled Johanna into her arms and hugged her. "Thank you so much!"

Johanna tightened her arms around her. "You're welcome, sweetheart."

Emma was the first to pull away. Johanna avoided her gaze and started the car. In silence she pulled the car onto the main road. "Thanks for agreeing to hang out with me today," she said.

"It's no problem. You're pretty cool."

Johanna smiled. "I'm glad you think so."

Maggie walked into Nancy's office and sat in the visitor's chair. She propped her feet up in the chair beside her and stared at the ceiling. Nancy looked up from her computer. "What's wrong, darling?" she asked.

"Who says anything is wrong?"

"Your body language says it all."

Maggie glanced at her from the corner of her eye. "It's Jo."

"What about her?"

"We just had an argument. Via text if you can believe that."

"What was it about?"

Maggie leaned back further in her chair and stared at the ceiling. "Emma's been with us for over a week and she hasn't told her yet. I was just trying to urge her to come clean, but she snapped on me. I'm just worried about her."

"Worried?"

"I'm worried that the stress is getting to her."

Nancy got up and came around her desk. She nudged Maggie's feet out of the chair and sat down beside her.

"I understand your worries, but Jo is strong. You know that. She's gotten through a lot worse."

"Yeah, but nothing like this has ever happened to her before. I think she's going to lose it." Maggie pulled her phone from her jacket pocket. "Look how she responded to me. This isn't her at all."

Nancy took the phone and scrolled through the messages. She shook her head slowly. "Maggie, honey. Try putting yourself into her shoes."

"I have."

"Have you really?"

Maggie got up and walked to the window. "Everything that I do I always consider her. Do you know what it's like living in fear every day?"

"In fear of what?"

Maggie leaned against the window. "I'm afraid that something will happen that'll make her snap and our sweet and kind Jo will disappear on us again."

Nancy joined her at the window. An afternoon rainstorm brewed on the horizon. "You've got to give her more credit than that."

"She's my best friend! Of course, I give her credit."

"That's not what I mean," Nancy said softly.

"Then what do you mean?"

Nancy turned Maggie to face her. "We need to be patient. Jo is under an immense amount of stress right now."

"I know."

"She will do what's right. I know she will."

Maggie shook her head slowly. "She told me that Emma's leaving town tomorrow sometime. Do you think she's going to tell her the truth?"

"Yes, I do."

"I just hope she doesn't relapse. She's been doing good for so long. I just don't understand why this girl had to show up now of all times."

Nancy shrugged. "Maybe because it was time."

The two women watched the distant storm in silence. After a few short minutes, Maggie decided to leave. She paused at the door.

"For the record, I do have faith in Jo, but I'm just scared. I'm afraid that she won't tell Emma the truth and then Emma's going to leave. And then Jo won't know how to cope with it."

Nancy nodded slowly.

"We almost didn't get her back last time. And I'm just afraid of it all happening again, but this time our Jo won't come back."

"I understand."

"I really hope you're right about this one."

Nancy sighed and took her seat at her desk. "Me too."

Without saying another word, Maggie left Nancy's office. Nancy stared at the door for a few minutes before she went back to working on the computer.

Johanna got out of the Jeep and peeked out from underneath the gas station awning. They'd pulled into an abandoned gas station when the rainstorm became too heavy to drive in. Johanna couldn't see well in the rain and she didn't feel like putting them in jeopardy by pushing through to the Ridge.

She hopped back inside the Jeep and sighed. "I can see it clearing up ahead, so it won't be much longer now," she said.

"If it's clearing up, why can't you just drive through it?" Emma asked.

"Well, because I can't see to drive when it's raining like this."

"Okay," Emma said looking out the window. "Man, this place is creepy. Are you sure it's safe sitting here?"

"Yes."

"Are you sure? It looks like a psycho could jump out at any minute and kill us."

THE MISSING PIECE

Johanna laughed. "Sorry to disappoint you, but there aren't any murderers in Bridger. You're safe here."

"That you know of. For all you know your cop boyfriend could be a serial killer."

Johanna chuckled and glanced out the window. "He's not my boyfriend."

"He's cute, I must admit, but he's too cute."

"Too cute?"

"Yeah, like extremely handsome model citizen by day, serial killer by night."

Johanna laughed and reclined her seat. "I can assure you that Paul is no serial killer. He's very sweet. Caring. He's a true gentleman."

Emma scoffed. "There's no such thing as a true gentleman."

"Of course, there is."

"I thought I had myself one of those," Emma sighed. "But he turned out to be a jerk."

Johanna looked over at her and smiled sympathetically. "Another will come along. You're a beautiful young woman with some wonderful qualities. It's only a matter of time before someone better comes along and snatches you up."

"You're just saying that," Emma said as she copied Johanna and reclined her seat.

"No, I'm not."

"Well, thanks. It's nice to hear someone old say that about me."

"Old? Seriously? I'm not old."

"Sorry, no offense. What are you? Like sixty or something?"

Johanna's mouth dropped open. "You're way off. I'm only fifty-two."

"Oh, I'm sorry."

They shared a laugh. Johanna glanced up at the sky. Just a few more minutes and the storm would be clearing up. She noticed Emma holding her stomach.

"Are you okay?"

"Yeah, just a little uncomfortable."

"I'm sorry about the delay. We should be moving soon."

"No problem." Emma noticed how jittery Johanna was. "Do I make you nervous?"

"No. Why do you ask?"

"I've noticed that every time I'm around you, you act nervous."

"Oh." Johanna laughed a little. "No, it's not that at all. I'm a nervous person by nature."

Emma nodded and leaned back in her seat. The rain poured in buckets outside. She didn't know where they were going, but she doubted she'd enjoy hiking around in the mud. She knew she shouldn't have agreed to come with her. She closed her eyes and listened to the sound of the rain falling on the hardtop.

"Tell me what your life is like in Chicago," Johanna said softly.

Emma was glad that Johanna broke the uncomfortable silence. It was starting to unnerve her. She laughed a little, opening one eye to glance at her.

"Always busy. Nothing like this."

"Do you like it here?"

"There's nothing to do here. No malls, no restaurants. I don't understand how you guys live here."

"It's not that bad. It's very quiet, true, but there's something about the peace and tranquility here that makes me happy."

Emma sighed and readjusted herself in the seat. "Chicago is fast paced. I have a job, but I really don't like it. I just do it because it pisses off my mom."

Johanna chuckled. "Most mothers like it when their kids have jobs."

"Not this one."

"Why not?"

Emma wasn't sure if she wanted to talk about Ericka. Life with her was depressing enough without having to talk about her. She chewed on her lip and crossed her arms over her chest.

"She thinks my job is beneath me, something that someone of our social status should not be doing." She opened her eyes and stared at the ceiling. "I'm a cashier at a grocery store," she added before Johanna could ask the question.

"What's wrong with that?"

"I asked her that question so many times I got tired of asking. She's just ashamed of me." Johanna didn't respond. Emma knew that she was waiting for her to continue. She doesn't know how she did it, but Johanna tricked her into talking about herself.

"Why is she ashamed of you?" she prodded.

Emma felt the tears stinging the backs of her eyes. Every time she thought about Ericka's rejection, she couldn't control the emotions simmering beneath the surface. She inhaled a deep breath and steadied herself.

"I guess I didn't turn out the way she wanted me to."

"You seem fine to me."

Emma laughed to stop herself from crying. "Thanks. I'm glad someone thinks so."

Johanna reached out and touched her gently on the shoulder. "You're a remarkably strong young woman. For you to have gone through what you just went through and be here with me right now shows how strong you are." Her voice was soft and reassuring.

"Mom didn't even care, you know."

Johanna nodded and squeezed her shoulder.

"What you heard on the phone is how she's with me all the time. Cold, judgmental, and uptight."

"Are you the only child?"

"Yes. Mom's got some ovary problem. She can't have kids so her and Dad adopted me. I was a charity case, I guess. They must have known I was born addicted to drugs."

"Has she always treated you this way?" Johanna asked.

"Yes, mostly. I remember being really little and getting kisses from her, but then one day she stopped. And I couldn't understand why."

"Did you ever ask her?"

"No. I was too afraid of the answer. I thought I'd done something wrong."

"I'm so sorry."

"It's okay. Once she got into the habit of giving me the cold shoulder, it never ended. She hated everything I did. Hated all my friends. All my boyfriends. It was terrible."

Johanna squeezed Emma's shoulder. "You deserve to be loved."

"I'm starting to wonder if that's true. Seems like every time I turn around, people who're supposed to love me, leave me." Emma cleared the emotion from her throat and straightened up. "What's wrong with me?"

"Nothing," Johanna whispered. "Nothing at all."

Emma turned her gaze out the window. The storm had slowed down to a light rain shower now. It seemed like the heavens opened up just long enough for her to pour out her heart to Johanna.

"Looks like it's about to stop raining," Emma said.

"Yeah, looks like it."

"I hate to do this, but I'm not feeling much like hiking right now."

Johanna nodded. "Okay."

"Is it early enough in the day for me to take a nap? And we can go to your special place later?"

"Yes. We can do that."

"I promise I still want to go, but I'm just bummed out now. Talking about my life depresses me."

"I understand," Johanna said with a smile and started the Jeep. She pulled up to the road and turned in the direction headed back to her place.

She said nothing the entire way back to her house. For thirty straight minutes, Johanna sat quietly and stared ahead. Emma wondered if she'd offended her. When they pulled into Johanna's driveway, Johanna quickly hopped out and went inside. Emma followed closely behind.

THE MISSING PIECE

Once inside Emma found her in the kitchen. She was digging through the freezer.

"I swear if she ate all of my ice cream, I'm going to kill her," Johanna said as she rummaged through the freezer case.

Emma took a seat at the island and laughed. "Best friends are notorious for stuff like that."

Johanna mumbled something and then resurfaced with a half-gallon container of ice cream. "She's sneaky. She tried to hide it from me."

"What flavor?"

"Fudge ripple."

"Yum."

"Would you like some?"

"I'd love some."

Johanna retrieved two bowls from the cupboard and divided the remaining ice cream between the two of them. She handed Emma a spoon and sat down beside her. She ate her ice cream in silence.

Emma copied her and ate her ice cream in silence. So many thoughts rushed through her head, thoughts that she couldn't understand completely. She wanted to leave town, but at the same time she wanted to stay. She wanted to disappear, but she also had an obligation to attend the fall gala.

And then thoughts about her birth mother swarmed around in her head. Thoughts of why she hadn't tried to see her, thoughts of what could be the big secret, and thoughts of why everyone was protecting her identity. She'd been here with Johanna and Maggie for days and Maggie hadn't said one thing about her, not even in casual conversation with Johanna. How is that possible if she's supposed to be best friends with Jane Doe? What kind of a best friend would—

No, she had to be processing this all wrong. Her mind scanned through everything that she'd been told since she arrived in Bridger, replaying every word that it recorded. From the basics that Nancy told her about Jane Doe to the intimate details that Johanna shared.

"Oh my God," she gasped and stood on shaky legs. She felt faint. She couldn't process the thoughts running through her mind. The answer was right in front of her the entire time. It all made sense now.

Johanna finished off the rest of her ice cream and placed the spoon down. She turned to face her; their eyes locked for the first real time since they've met.

"You're her," Emma whispered. She grabbed hold of the edge of the island to steady herself. "Aren't you?"

Johanna sighed. "Yes. I am."

THE MISSING PIECE

"I don't understand," Emma said, sitting back down in her chair. The room spun slowly. "Why didn't you tell me?"

"I was going to tell you today."

"Why today? Why not when we first met?"

"I wasn't ready."

"You weren't ready? What about me?"

"I understand you're upset, Emma, but—"

"But what? How can you possibly explain any of this?"

"I wanted to wait, so I'd be sure."

"You wanted to be sure of what?" She choked on the lump in her throat. "Did you want to be sure that I was good enough for you?" She felt the tears stinging the backs of her eyes and she silently cursed herself for showing emotion this soon.

"No. God, no Emma."

"Then what?" She couldn't control the emotions boiling to the surface. Knowing that she was here with her birth mother the entire time and not revealing herself felt like the ultimate rejection.

She stared at this woman who'd become a friend to her. She'd grown to trust and confide in her. How could she do this?

"How could you do this?" she asked.

"I'm sorry, Emma. I know I should've told you sooner, but I was afraid."

"Afraid of what?" She laughed lightly but it was only to stop herself from crying. The pain she felt was different than anything she'd felt before. "Oh my God, you're my mother?"

Johanna nodded. "Yes, I am."

Emma gripped her stomach as a wave of nausea washed over her. "So, you knew all along, didn't you?" It was more a statement than a question.

"Yes."

"But I don't understand why you didn't tell me. Why wouldn't you allow the others to tell me?"

"It's long and complicated. I... I—" Johanna stumbled over her words. "I was shocked. I didn't expect you to ever show up in my life."

"Didn't you think that one day your kid might show up looking for you?"

Johanna shook her head slowly. "No. I didn't think it was possible."

"Why not?"

Johanna got up and went to the fridge. She grabbed a container of leftovers and opened it. She ignored Emma's question and nibbled on the dessert cake from the previous night. Emma noticed that Johanna's hands trembled more now, and she was having difficulty holding the container. But she kept standing by the fridge, eating quietly.

"Will you answer me, please?" Emma said softer. Emma could see that Johanna was under a lot of stress. Maybe it was anxiety, but whatever it was, she recognized that she inherited her nervous eating habit from her mother.

Her mother...

The realization set in that she was actually sitting in her birth mother's kitchen watching her pig out on cake. She'd found her. She actually found her. Johanna groaned under her breath and faced her.

"I didn't deserve it," she said quietly. "After what I put you through, I didn't deserve the privilege of having you in my life, so I just accepted that and let go."

"You didn't know you were pregnant with me, right?"

"Right. How lame is that?" she laughed a little and went over to the sink and washed the container clean. "I was a horrible mother from the start."

"Don't say that."

"I wanted to keep you, you know. In my crazy messed up mind, I thought I could make it right. I thought I could get clean and do the right thing. But when they told me you were struggling to live and would most likely die, it killed me inside."

Emma was speechless.

"I wasn't a person of prayer, but I prayed to whoever might've been listening and I asked them to please get you through it. I promised that if you got through it, I'd do whatever I needed to do to make things right."

"But you gave me up."

"I didn't give you up. The State took you from me." Johanna's voice suddenly turned cold. "I wanted so badly to make it up to you, but they wouldn't let me." She turned away from Emma when her tears came to the surface. "They wouldn't let me," she repeated.

Emma was about to respond, but Maggie came through the door carrying two handfuls of groceries bags. Almost immediately she noticed that she'd walked into a tense situation. Johanna quickly swiped away her tears and helped her with the bags.

"You're home early," she said grabbing a set of bags from Maggie's left arm.

"Yeah," she replied, glancing over at Emma. "I thought you two were going to be gone all day. I was going to have a party."

Johanna chuckled and busied herself putting away the groceries.

Emma sat at the island, too afraid to move. She wanted more from Johanna. She was irritated that Maggie had come in when she did. She was sure it was written all over her face. She tried to hold in her tears but the longer she sat and watched Johanna, the more she wanted answers.

"What am I supposed to do now?" Emma asked.

Johanna stopped what she was doing and turned around. "I don't know, Emma. What do you want to do?"

"I want to leave and never look back," she forced out. A part of her meant it and a part of her didn't. "You did me wrong and you know it."

Johanna nodded. "I know. And I'm sorry."

"Sorry can't fix this, Johanna. I mean, did you think I was going to judge you or something?"

"Yes."

"That's crazy! I was the one who came looking for you, remember? But you tricked me. You all tricked me." She looked over at Maggie and was met with an intense expression. "Every one of you was a party to a lie."

"We weren't lying, Emma. It was my responsibility to tell you, not theirs."

"I get that, but this whole thing is crazy, and I don't want to be a part of it. Just so you know, you don't have to entertain me any longer. I'll pack my things today and leave for home tonight."

"I thought you still wanted to go to the Ridge with me."

"That was before I realized that you were my mother!" Emma knew the words sliced through Johanna's heart, but it was too late to take them back.

Johanna turned away from her and finished putting away the groceries. Maggie placed the rest of the bags down on the counter and walked over to Johanna. She put her arm around her and whispered something to her. She glanced over her shoulder at Emma, giving her a fierce look of displeasure. After a moment, Johanna responded by leaving Maggie alone with Emma.

Emma wasn't intimidated. She'd say the same things to Maggie that she'd said to Johanna. She didn't care. She was tired of being manipulated and lied to. Maggie came and sat down next to Emma. Her face had softened a bit. She tapped her fingers lightly on the countertop.

"Do you feel better?" Maggie asked.

"Better?"

"You came all this way looking for her. You found her. And then you shoved a knife through her heart. Do you feel better?"

"I did no such thing."

"Do you think it was easy for her to tell you?"

Emma laughed. "Actually, she didn't tell me. I figured it out on my own!"

"Well, congrats. Remind me to give you a prize later."

"What's your problem?"

"My problem, if you call it that, is that you came here looking for your mother and you found her. Why can't you be happy about that?"

Maggie irritated her so much right now. She wanted to tell her how she really felt, but she held back her words.

"Jo has come an awful long way for some spoiled brat to come along and mess that up for her."

"Spoiled brat?"

"Yeah, I know all about you and your high-class family. I know all about your perfect parents who can do no wrong. I've done my research. If all you want to do is punish her for giving you up, then you need to just pack your bags and get the hell out of my house."

"I'm not trying to punish her."

"Jo is a good woman. She'll give the shirt off her back to anyone and I'm not going to let you hurt her. Do you understand that? She's come too far."

"You don't have to worry about me. I'll be leaving tomorrow." She narrowed her eyes, intent on holding the gaze of the most intimidating woman she'd ever met. And she thought Ericka was tough.

Maggie stared at her for a moment, her intense glare eventually melting into a soft laugh. "God, you're just like her," she said as she got up and finished putting away the groceries. She had nothing else to say to Emma. She'd made her point.

Emma rolled her eyes and looked away. She didn't want to talk anymore. She just wanted to disappear for a while. When she was certain that Maggie wasn't going to say anything else, she took the opportunity to escape out of the room.

Emma stirred her coffee, staring vacantly into the cup. It was probably cold by now, but she didn't feel like asking Vicks for another fresh cup. She was tired of sitting in this booth. Her body ached and all she wanted was to lay down and get some sleep before the long drive ahead of her.

It was the right thing to do. She'd already disrupted Johanna's life enough. She questioned whether she should've started searching in the first place. She'd found her and before she realized Johanna was her mother, she actually liked her. But now she was angry with her. Angry at her for keeping her in the dark. Angry at her because she knew all along but had said nothing.

Her thoughts traveled to when she was in the hospital and the sickening conversation that she had with Ericka. She couldn't believe how many disappointments she'd had in the last few weeks. She thought being dumped by Cal was the most heartbreaking, but as she contemplated having found Johanna and then leaving her tomorrow, she was sure that this was the most hurtful.

Her phone buzzed on the table. She glanced down to see Lexie calling. She sighed heavily, not really wanting to talk to anyone at the moment. She knew if she didn't answer, she'd keep calling all night. She swiped the phone off the table and answered.

"Hey Lex, what's up?"

"What's going on with you, Em?"

"What do you mean?"

"I haven't heard from you in days. Do I have to come there? Is there something wrong?"

"No, you don't have to come here. Nothing other than what you already know is wrong."

"Em, mentally, are you okay? You're handling the miscarriage pretty well."

Emma shrugged and ran her fingers through her hair. "I'm okay. I don't want to think about it or talk about it if you don't mind."

Lexie went silent for a while. "Did you find your mother?"

Emma didn't want to talk about that either. "Yes, I did. In fact, she was—" she caught herself before she divulged that Johanna had sat with her at the hospital and held her hand through the worst part of the process. At the time, Emma was thankful that she didn't have to go through it alone, even if Johanna was a stranger.

She swallowed the lump in her throat and groaned. Johanna was there for her. She'd stayed all night, right by her side. She only got up once to go to the bathroom, but besides that, she was constantly at her side. Every time Emma opened her eyes, she saw Johanna's staring back at her. It was the most comforting feeling she'd ever felt in her life. She found comfort in her mother's eyes.

"She was what?" Lexie asked.

Emma struggled to keep her composure. "Nothing, Lex. I'm going to be heading home soon. I'll text you when I'm on the road."

"Em, please."

"Please what?"

"Please tell me what's happened? You're not the same anymore."

Emma laughed. "Hmm, let's see. Cal dumped me when I chose our child over him, only to miscarry it later." Her voice quavered with emotion. It still hurt to say it. "And then, when I told Ericka, she basically told me I deserved what I got."

"Geesh! Your mother said that?"

"Right now, I don't even want you to call her that. Ericka has hurt me for the last time."

"I'm sorry, Em."

Johanna's face flashed through her mind. She thought about when she first spent the time with her at

Charlotte's House and how much she enjoyed her company. She thought about how impressed she was when she observed how every one of the women residents interacted with her. She was well loved and highly respected. And she was so gentle and kind. She thought of the night she was in the hospital and how several times that night she caught herself wishing that Ericka was more like Johanna.

"I met my real mother and she's an amazing woman. Everyone seems to like her," Emma said.

"I hear a but coming," Lexie said.

"Nah, no buts. There's a lot more to this story but I don't want to talk about her right now. It's just a lot for me to absorb."

"I understand."

"You don't really. But I wish you did."

"Do you need me to fly out there and be with you, because you know I will."

Emma smiled. "Yeah, I know you wouldn't hesitate to come if I needed you, but I'm fine."

"All right. I guess I'll have to be happy with that."

"You've got no choice."

They shared a laugh. It felt good to laugh through her pain. She loved Lexie and their friendship, but she didn't want to go back to Chicago. She wanted to head west and never look back. Ericka only wanted her to return so she could showcase her like she'd done for the past twenty-two years. Ericka made it a career out of showing her philanthropic acts, the highest one being adopting Emma, a drug addicted baby.

Emma was tired of the façades that she'd put on just so her parents could rake in the dough. She was just tired. She needed change.

"I've gotta go, Em. I'm training a new girl today."

"Oh, that sounds like fun."

"Not!"

Emma chuckled and held the phone. "I'll talk to you later."

"Great. Hey, I just wanna say that I'm so happy you found your real mom. You deserve so much happiness and I hope she's all, if not more, than you've ever hoped for."

"Thanks, Lex. Bye." She didn't wait for Lexie to respond before disconnecting the call. Her last statement suddenly overwhelmed her. Johanna was nothing like Ericka. She'd be doing her an injustice by comparing them on equal scales. She felt her chest swelling up with so much emotion that it hurt to breathe. She checked the time. She took a sip of her cold coffee and placed a twenty-dollar bill on the table. She'd been gone long enough. It was time to face Johanna so she could get on with her life.

Emma had gone back to the house to speak to Johanna, but the only person she found was Maggie. It took some persuading but eventually Emma got her to tell her where Johanna had gone. Before she revealed her whereabouts, she made Emma promise not to go after her just to start another argument.

Johanna had gone to her favorite spot, Eagle's Ridge. It's where she always went when she was stressed out and wanted to relax. It was her comfort zone. Maggie scribbled down the directions and sent Emma on her way.

The entire way there, Emma tried to think of reasons to turn back, but she couldn't come up with anything. She couldn't have turned around even if she tried. She was drawn to her, and as much as she wanted to run away in the opposite direction, she couldn't. At least not yet.

The parking space was easy to find, literally only one turn off of the main road that led out of Bridger. She pulled into the space next to Johanna's jeep and got out. She looked around. There wasn't a soul in sight. Ahead of her was a trail that twisted and winded around the back side of the hill.

THE MISSING PIECE

She glanced down at the directions, read them several times, and then set off. Five minutes into the hike, she wished she had worn more comfortable shoes. The trail was arduous for an inexperienced trail hiker like her, but she pushed forward. It was hot, she was sweating profusely, her legs cramped, but she wasn't going to turn back now.

She came to a high point and noticed a fork in the trail. She pulled out the directions.

"At the fork, go left," she said to herself. She looked to her left. The trail ascended higher and curved out of sight. "You gotta be kidding me," she lamented.

She looked to the right. That footpath descended down towards a small lake. She laughed to herself.

"That figures. It couldn't have been that easy."

She took the trail left and ascended the Ridge. Emma lost track of time viewing the beautiful scenery around her. She'd never seen so much beauty in one place before. All her life, she'd only seen skyscrapers and manufactured beauty. Nothing like this.

Her walk up the trail became less of a hike and more of a stroll. She was actually enjoying it. When she topped the hill, she referred back to the directions. According to them, she'd made it to Eagle's Ridge. She looked around for Johanna, looking in every possible direction. She'd almost given up when she saw Johanna off to her left, sitting on a bench. Emma walked towards her, being careful not to disturb her thoughts. She approached quietly and stood at a close distance behind her. She followed her gaze and discovered the same breathtaking image that Johanna had painted on her canvas at home. She couldn't believe her eyes.

She took a moment to catch her breath. "It looks much better in person," Emma said softly.

Johanna gasped and spun around in her seat. She stared at Emma as if she were seeing an apparition. Her mouth hung open, but she said nothing.

"You okay?" Emma asked.

"I... Um, yeah. I'm fine," she said. She scooted over and turned back to admire the view.

Emma sat down with a heavy sigh next to her. She clasped her hands together in her lap and noticed that Johanna was sitting in the same position, with her hands resting comfortably in her lap.

"How did you find me?" Johanna asked. She kept her eyes on the view in front of her as if she was expecting something spectacular to happen.

"Maggie gave me directions."

Johanna scoffed and folded her arms across her chest. "When are you leaving?"

"Probably tomorrow if I can get a good night's rest."

"All right." Johanna swallowed hard and adjusted herself on the bench. "Please be careful, okay?"

"Yeah," Emma said quietly. She turned toward Johanna and sighed. "Johanna?"

"Yes, Emma."

"Would you look at me, please?"

Johanna hesitated, but eventually she gave in to Emma's request. Her eyes were red, and her face tear streaked. "Yes, Emma," she repeated.

"Can we talk for a minute?"

"What would you like to talk about?"

"First, I want to apologize for the way I talked to you earlier. I was just surprised, and it's hard for me to process a lot of different emotions at one time."

"I can understand that."

"I'm not a hurtful person like that. So, I'm sorry. But you've got to understand where I'm coming from, too. How would you feel if you were me?"

"I'd probably feel the same way," she answered quietly.

Emma was surprised with Johanna's manner. Even when she was obviously upset, she was still calm and laid back. Perhaps this is how she was all the time.

"Are you angry with me?" Emma asked.

"You had every right to be upset and I deserved it."

"I just wish I would've expressed myself differently. I didn't mean to hurt you."

Johanna reached for her hand. "None of that matters now, okay?" She gave her hand a little squeeze. "Let's just enjoy the time we have together. How about that?"

Emma stared at her in confusion. "Oh, okay." She tightened her grip on Johanna's hand and sat back on the bench. The rays from the afternoon sun warmed and invigorated her.

She glanced down at their joined hands. Johanna held hers like it was something she did every day. She didn't seem to have a second thought about it. Emma, however, was nearly squirming in her seat. She wasn't used to this. She'd never experienced this type of maternal affection before. She never knew what it was like to be held and comforted by her mother. This was new. Johanna noticed Emma gazing at her tattoo.

She smiled and squeezed Emma's hand. "After I'd given birth to you, I saw you for a split second. But in that brief moment, I fell in love with you. I couldn't believe that you came out of me." She laughed nervously and continued. "I was completely shocked, but in my crazy mind, I thought I was going to keep you. So, I gave you a name."

"What did you name me?"

She turned her forearm so Emma could be reminded of the name she asked about earlier. "I named you Mila."

"Mila?"

"Yes. It's means a miracle. And that's what you are. You're a living, breathing miracle."

"Wow." Emma couldn't bring herself to say anything more. All of this was surreal. She was finding out things about herself that she never thought possible.

Johanna chuckled softly and released Emma's hand. "I really thought I could care for you, but when they informed me that you were born addicted and was suffering severe withdrawals, I felt horrible. I felt like a failure."

"Did you get to see me anytime later?"

"No. I tried to. I even resorted to begging but they looked at me with judgmental eyes. I'd ruined my life and ruined yours before it even got started. I'm so thankful for Nance and Mags for being there for me. It was really hard."

"Who looked at you through judgmental eyes? Nancy and Maggie?"

"No. The hospital staff were also people I went to school with and dealt with on a daily basis prior to my bad years. By the time I showed up at the hospital, I was terribly addicted to opioids. I'd done some pretty terrible things that all of town knew about."

"What kind of things?"

Johanna shook her head and looked away. "The kind of things a daughter would be ashamed of if she knew her mother did them."

"I'm not ashamed of you. No matter what it was."

Johanna turned back to face her. "Do you mean that?"

"Yes," Emma said scooting closer. "I'm over the initial shock. I just want to get to know you."

"I googled you," Johanna said with a soft laugh. "Your parents are really impressive. And your mother... Wow. She seems so outgoing and a people person."

"None of that matters."

"I'm nothing like her."

"I'm glad you're not," Emma said quickly. "Please, I need to hear this from you."

Johanna sighed lightly. "All right. I'll spare you the sordid details but let's just say when I got really bad into the pain killers, my habit became insatiable. I needed more at whatever cost. I'd buy them from people, steal them from friends, and eventually I sunk lower and lower into a depraved way of life. All the while, I was humiliating my family by my actions. But I didn't care. I just didn't want to feel the pain."

"Oh man."

THE MISSING PIECE

"I was in and out of Redemption Valley, but when I had you, I promised myself I was done, and I'd do whatever I needed to do to get and stay clean."

"But what happened? Why couldn't you keep me if you wanted to?"

Johanna groaned and crossed her arms across her chest. "The case worker who was sent out from the county was someone that I'd hurt by my actions a year earlier. I met this guy and did what I had to do to get some cash for some drugs. Turns out, that guy was this lady's husband." Johanna shook her head slowly. "Her family fell apart because of me."

Emma touched her lightly on the leg. "If her family fell apart, it was because of her cheating husband. Not you."

Johanna smiled at her and shrugged. "When she appeared at the door, I knew I was in trouble. I thought that it was God's way of punishing me for what I'd done to her." Johanna got up from the bench and paced in front of Emma. "No matter what I told her, she wouldn't let me keep you. She said that there was no guarantee that I'd stay clean enough to take care of you properly. She said she was doing what was best for you, but deep down I knew she also wanted to hurt me as much as I had hurt her."

"Then what happened?"

"She was from the child protective services. I couldn't fight them when you were born the way you were because of me. I was deemed unfit. Case closed."

Emma took a moment to process all of that. She saw the pain that Johanna was reliving as she recounted the time of her birth. It gave her a renewed sense of hope knowing how much Johanna wanted to keep her.

"If you'd kept me, would we still live here?"

Johanna laughed softly. "Either that or I would've packed us up and headed west."

"West, huh. That's funny."

Johanna leaned against the railing and went silent. She zoned out for a few minutes thinking about whatever it was that she was thinking of. Everything about her was so appealing to Emma. She liked her a lot.

"I wanted a tattoo once. When I was a junior in high school," Emma said.

"Oh really?"

"Yeah, but my mom squashed that idea. A Benson would never do such a thing, she'd always say."

Johanna laughed in response. "What about now?"

"Oh, no. I don't like pain. That's why the thought of childbirth really freaked me out." Emma sighed heavily and leaned back on the bench. "I guess I'm off the hook about that now."

Johanna watched her for a moment before she came and sat down beside her. She put her arm around her and pulled her closer. "When you get back home, make sure you take some time for yourself, okay?"

"I wish I could do that, but I've got to go back to work, and we have this fall gala coming up that my family is hosting."

"It's really important to give yourself time to come to terms."

"I'm fine."

"Your mouth says one thing, but your eyes say another."

Emma lowered her head and groaned. Of course, Johanna could see through her. She avoided her gaze, fixing her eyes on the view in front of them.

"I'm going to be fine. The only thing I'm concerned about is running into Cal."

"Who is Cal?"

"He's my ex. The one who dumped me when I told him I was pregnant."

"Oh, I see."

"Right now, I'm so angry with him. I'm not sure what I'll do if I see his face again anytime soon."

"I understand."

Emma held back her angry tears and took deep and steadying breaths. Although Johanna had seen her at her most vulnerable, in the hospital, she didn't want to be this exposed right now. She didn't want her to see that she'd hinged her happiness on a man she didn't really know. Cal probably only wanted to be with her because she was a Benson. Just like all the rest of them.

"Thank you for staying with me at the hospital," Emma whispered. "You don't know how much that means to me."

"I think I do," she said.

Emma took another deep and cleansing breath. She fought a losing battle against her will to keep her composure and her need to purge her soul. She tried hard to keep the tears at bay, but the tenderness of her mother's touch made it harder and harder to control. When she was no longer able to hold it back, she covered her face and broke down.

Johanna pulled her into a tight embrace. "I'm so sorry," she whispered.

Emma cried for her broken and failed relationships with Ericka and Cal, for the missed opportunity to be a mother, and everything else she'd held inside over the years.

"Shh," Johanna consoled her. "You're safe. Just let it out," she whispered.

Emma did exactly that and let it all out. She cried for the first real time in the arms of someone who truly cared about her. Johanna became her safe space. Emma cried until she couldn't cry anymore.

"I'm sorry," she said pulling away from Johanna and sitting up. "That's not how I wanted our conversation to go."

"It's all right."

Emma glanced down at her watch. "I guess I should be getting back to the house if I'm going to get some sleep."

Johanna nodded but didn't say anything.

"Could we take a picture together? Just so I'll have it with me?" Emma asked.

"Yes, I'd like that." Johanna hopped up and stood with her back to the scenic view. "This is the perfect backdrop, right?"

Emma smiled and came to her side. She put her arm around her and snapped a selfie with her."

"Thank you. I'm so glad I found you."

"I'm glad you found me, too." Johanna started walking slowly back down the trail, cherishing every last minute she had with her.

Instead of following her, Emma sat back down and admired the view one last time. It was etched into her memory. She'd never forget this place, nor the things that happened to her. She smiled and looked back over her shoulder to see how far Johanna had gotten.

Johanna was standing close, smiling warmly at her. She waited for Emma to join her and when Emma came to her side, Johanna hugged her tightly. "Let's get you back to the house so you can rest up," she said with a smile.

"All right."

"I'll make you a nice dinner before you go to bed. How does that sound?"

"Sounds great. Thank you."

"Anything for you," she said.

Emma slipped her arm in Johanna's and they walked together down the trail to their vehicles, both knowing they would never forget this moment.

16

Johanna had just put the last dish into the dishwasher when Maggie came into the kitchen. She avoided her eyes because Maggie would see through her façade. She couldn't stand the thought of Emma leaving, not after spending so much time with her. But who was she to ask her to stay? She had a life back home in Chicago. A better one. A life where she'd never be in want of anything.

Who was she to ask her to stay in Bridger and sacrifice the luxuries that she was used to? Johanna sighed heavily and tossed the hand towel on the countertop. She opened the fridge and pulled out a slice of lemon meringue pie.

"That's my slice," Maggie said as she took her seat at the island. "Hand it over."

"You've already eaten your slice. This was a leftover."

"My name's on it."

Johanna inspected the plate only to realize that she wasn't really serious. She chuckled and sat down at the island next to Maggie. She cut into the pie and started eating it slowly.

"You okay?" Maggie asked.

"Right now, I am. I'm not sure about when she leaves, though."

"I'm glad you two worked it out."

"Me, too," Johanna said, sad tears filling her eyes.

"You should pack her a lunch and some snacks for the road."

"Yeah." Johanna picked at her pie slice. She held back her tears. Everything that she'd been afraid of didn't happen. Emma didn't judge her, nor did she come to punish her for giving her up.

"Or you could make it easier on yourself by asking her to stay here with us."

Johanna whipped her head around. "What?"

Maggie shrugged. "Why don't you ask her to stay?"

"Here?"

"Yes," she said with a laugh.

"She'd never want to stay here with me. And plus, we don't have an extra room."

"I think she would. And if she wanted to, she could have the room above the garage. It just needs some cleaning and fixing up. We could get her to help us do it."

Johanna pondered over the idea for a moment. It would be nice to have Emma here, but that would be asking Emma to sacrifice too much. "I don't know, Mags."

"What could it hurt to ask?"

"What if she says no?"

"Then leave the door open for her to come back any time she wants to come and visit you."

Johanna sighed and stuffed another forkful of pie into her mouth. "I have nothing to give her," she whispered hotly. "She's been better off without me in her life. Why would I ask her to give all that up for me?"

Maggie reached over and covered Johanna's hand with her own. "Because I know you need her just as much as she needs you. It's obvious."

"What I need is for you to understand that I have to let her go back home."

"Why do you have to do that?"

"Because she's better off without me!"

"There you go saying that again. How do you know she's better off without you? Just because her adoptive family is wealthy?"

"Yes."

"You heard what the girl told us when she got here, Jo. None of that matters to her. All she wants is you. Materially, you can't give her what she's already got, but you have something that the other woman doesn't."

"What do I have?"

"You've got the love that belongs to her. You can't tell me that the moment you found out that she was your daughter, you didn't start feeling love for her."

Johanna looked away, gazing out of the window.

"Be honest, Jo. Didn't you love her the moment you knew?"

"Yes."

"And didn't that love for her grow the more you talked to her?"

Johanna nodded and wiped a tear from her eye. "Yes."

"If you didn't love that girl, you wouldn't have sat up there at the hospital all day and night by her side."

"I know, I know. What's your point?"

"My point is, stop fighting the truth. For once in your life accept the fact that good things can happen to you too, Jo. You're sitting here telling me that you can't give her as much as her adoptive parents have given her. Materially, that may be so, but there's one thing that Emma's been missing all these years. That's her mother's love... And only you can give that to her. You're what she's been missing."

Johanna nodded, acknowledging the truthfulness of Maggie's words. "I don't deserve her," she whispered. The tears choked her words as she tried her best to get her point across. "She was taken from me because I was too screwed up to be what she needed."

"But what about now? Are you screwed up now?"

"Yes!"

"No, you're not." Maggie sighed and took Johanna's trembling hands, stilling them. "Do you know what today is?"

"Of course, I know what today is."

"Your daughter showed up on your doorstep almost seven years to the day of you getting clean. That's no coincidence, Jo," she said softly. "I see it for what it really is even if you refuse to."

"What do you see, Mags?"

Maggie reached over and wiped the tears out of Johanna's eyes. "All these years you've been blaming yourself for what happened."

Johanna nodded. "I know."

"If you had known that you were pregnant back then, I know you wouldn't have kept using. You would've come back to Redemption and got help. I know you would've."

"I wish I could go back."

"Don't wish that. You were a terrible person back then."

Johanna chuckled. "Gee thanks, Mags."

"We both were, and you know it. We were controlled by the drugs. We had no control over our own lives. Now we do. Don't ever wish to go back."

"I just wish that I could go back and change how it all happened. Then maybe she'd be with me now."

"Don't you get it, Jo? You've been given a second chance because she's right here, right now, and your pride is about to let her walk out of your life."

"This isn't as easy as you make this out to be. There's a lot at stake!"

"Yeah, there's a lot at stake, all right, but they're not the things you're thinking of."

"What do you mean by that?"

"I hope you figure that out before it's too late." Maggie got up and placed a supportive hand on Johanna's shoulder. "I really do," she offered more softly.

Johanna just stared at her, unsure of how to respond.

"What time's dinner?"

"A little earlier today. Around five."

"All right. I'm going to grab a nap. I'll see you in a couple hours."

Johanna turned her back to her. There was too much running through her mind right now to carry on the conversation. Maggie disappeared out of the kitchen, leaving Johanna alone with her thoughts. Maggie was right. She was always right.

THE MISSING PIECE

She clenched her hands together to stop them from trembling. She had to do something before the feelings inside overwhelmed her. She put her face in her hands and nearly started crying on the spot. She had to gather herself before she broke apart completely. She'd come too far. Too far to mess up now.

She jumped out of her seat and rushed upstairs to talk to Emma, but she found her sleeping soundly on the couch. Johanna smiled and walked over to her. She removed Emma's shoes and covered her with a blanket. She leaned down and placed a tender kiss on Emma's forehead.

"I love you," she whispered. She stroked Emma's hair and watched her for a minute before getting up and disappearing into her studio.

She had to channel the feelings that now raged inside of her. They were unlike anything she'd ever experienced before. She couldn't even describe them properly, all she wanted to do was dull it. She didn't want to feel it at all. She squeezed her eyes tightly shut and took a deep and stabilizing breath.

"You've come too far to turn back now," she whispered to herself. After a few minutes, she opened her eyes and walked over to her easel.

With trembling hands, she picked up her paintbrush and stared at the unfinished picture on the canvas. She made her first brushstroke, and then her second. A smile peeked from the corner of her mouth. She worked for an hour straight, until she'd finished her painting. She never realized that her inspiration would appear like this. After so many months of sitting unfinished on the easel, she'd found what was missing.

17

Emma bolted from her sleep gasping for breath. She held her chest, trying her best to steady her racing heart. She looked around and it was dark. Grabbing her phone, she checked the time. It was going on 10pm.

"Oh crap," she groaned. She'd slept right through dinner with Johanna. She got up and stretched, looking around for either one of the women, but no one was in sight. Johanna's bedroom door was open, but the lights were off. She wasn't in there.

Emma got up and walked downstairs and looked for them in the kitchen. All that she found was a note Johanna left for her telling her that her dinner was in the microwave. Emma left the kitchen and explored the rest of the house. She came to Maggie's bedroom and knocked lightly.

Maggie answered the door. From the looks of it, she was already in bed.

"Hey, have you seen Johanna?" Emma asked.

"Not in about an hour or so. Check out back in her garden. She's probably there."

"Okay. Thanks. I'm sorry if I woke you."

"Nah, I wasn't sleeping yet. You okay, kid?"

Emma nodded, but she wasn't really sure. She felt a strange emotion in the center of her chest every time she thought about leaving. "I'm just going to miss you all."

"Aww. Just know that the feeling is mutual."

"Thanks."

"Please say goodbye in the morning before you leave."

"I was planning to leave early."

"No matter what time. I'd appreciate a goodbye."

"All right. Will do."

Maggie gave her a nod before she closed the door behind her. Emma went in search of Johanna and as Maggie had said, found her in her backyard garden. Johanna was lounging in the hammock gazing up at a clear and beautiful starry sky. The stars were bright tonight, sparkling almost like they were alive. Emma was amazed by how Johanna's eyes reflected the light of the stars, making her eyes twinkle.

Emma didn't want to disrupt her peace, but she knew this would probably be the last time she could speak to her alone before she left for home. Emma cleared her throat softly, trying not to startle her, but she still jumped anyway.

"Hey," Emma said.

Johanna turned her head towards her. "Hi."

THE MISSING PIECE

"I'm sorry I slept through dinner. I had every intention of coming, I just—"

"I understand," Johanna interrupted. "You needed your rest. Why are you up?"

"I just popped awake, I guess. I might be hungry."

Johanna laughed softly. "That's good. I put aside a plate for you. It's in the microwave."

"I saw your note. Thank you."

"Any time." Johanna's eyes lingered on Emma's for so long that they fell into an awkward silence.

Emma didn't know what to say. She realized that the reason why Johanna's eyes sparkled so much was because she had tears in them. And Emma wasn't prepared for this. Johanna wiped her tears away and focused her gaze back on the night sky.

Emma took a seat on the bench near Johanna's feet. "Are you okay?" she asked.

"Um hm."

Emma glanced over at her just as she was wiping more tears from her face. Johanna was so different from Ericka. More emotional. Ericka wouldn't be caught dead showing any kind of emotion like this. Emma wasn't sure how to react but seeing her like this made her want to hug her and ease whatever pain she was feeling. Her own heart tugged seeing Johanna in tears.

"I'll probably hit the road around four-thirty," Emma said.

"That's early."

"Yeah, it's better that way. For me at least."

Johanna didn't respond to her immediately, she just continued gazing up at the sky. "Please make sure you stay safe and you can text or call me if you get bored on the road."

"I would like that," Emma said. She'd been taught all of her life never to address someone else's emotions, but she really wanted to know why Johanna was like this. "Is there something wrong?"

"Nothing is wrong."

"Why are you crying then?" she asked.

"I'm just emotional, that's all."

"Why are you emotional?" Emma asked.

Johanna exhaled deeply. "I think you know the answer to that."

Emma thought about it for a minute. It couldn't be that. "Because I'm leaving?"

"Bingo."

This was all new to her. Having someone who actually showed emotion and cried over her. "I'll come back to visit."

It was then that Johanna turned to her. "Would you like to stay here with me?"

"Stay here? Like, live with you?"

"Yes."

Emma's mouth dropped open. If she was going to be honest, she'd thought about it on numerous occasions. The air was crisp, the land was wide open, the people were nice. While she was in bed recovering, she'd thought about learning to ride a horse and taking the horse up into the mountains. Although she'd never done it before, it seemed like it would be fun.

Her excitement faded as she thought about the Bensons and Chicago and the need to keep her word about the fall gala. Ericka expected her to come back and help with it. She didn't want to go back but she had to.

"I wish I could, but I'm needed to help out back home with the holiday season galas. The first one is the fall gala and then the winter and then New Year's…" Emma heard herself talking and all she heard was the sound of babble. For some reason she felt the need to explain how important these events were to the Bensons. Perhaps it was to ease the sting of her rejection of Johanna's offer.

Johanna listened quietly until Emma finished spieling. "I understand."

The way she said it seemed so final. How could she understand when Emma couldn't even understand what just came out of her own mouth?

"I'm sorry," Emma said.

"No worries."

Emma cursed herself inside. "Thank you again for all that you did for me. I could have never imagined it would turn out like this."

"It was my pleasure spending this time with you." Her voice betrayed the fact that she was on the verge of tears.

Emma lowered her head and cursed under her breath. She didn't know what else to say. Nothing that she could say now would make this situation feel any better. She'd found her mother and she was better than she expected. She was everything that Ericka was not. She was everything that Emma needed.

"I'll miss you," Emma whispered. She felt a lump rise into her throat making it extremely difficult to say anything more. She was glad that it was dark out, at least her tears could be hidden.

Johanna got up from the hammock and sat next to her on the bench. She pulled her into an embrace and held her tight. Emma buried her face into Johanna's shoulder and cherished the moment with her. She inhaled deeply, committing to memory the way her mother smelled and felt. The peace she felt when she was in Johanna's arms was the kind that she'd never felt prior to meeting her.

"You were right," Emma said. "It is the best feeling in the world."

Johanna whimpered and held her tighter. "I love you," she said.

"I love you, too." Emma held back her tears even though all she wanted to do was break down.

Johanna pulled away from her and replaced strands of Emma's hair that had been messed up by the hug. She smiled at her and picked tiny pieces of lint off of Emma's shirt. She sighed heavily and squeezed Emma's shoulders firmly.

"I'm going to go to bed, all right?"

Emma nodded, but kept silent.

"I'll see you in the morning before you leave," she said before placing a tender kiss on Emma's forehead.

Emma felt her trembling and when she pulled away, she got up and walked away quickly. Emma watched her disappear into the house. She didn't know how long she'd been sitting there before she eventually found it inside herself to go back inside and settle in for the night. It was nearing midnight before she had finished eating. The entire house was quiet. When she went upstairs to grab the rest of her bags she stopped by Johanna's door. She was sound asleep, snoring lightly.

She pressed her hand against the door and sighed heavily. She couldn't sleep now even if she tried. She'd decided to leave before they woke up. It would be easier that way. Doing it this way, she wouldn't have to worry about upsetting Johanna all over again.

She grabbed what was left of her things and tiptoed downstairs. After one last look around, she walked out, locking the door behind her. She didn't look back as she got in her car and drove away. The last thing she wanted to do was cause more hurt to the woman who'd gone through so much already. It was better this way...

18

Johanna walked into the kitchen rubbing the sleep out of her eyes. She dragged herself over to the coffee maker and flipped it on. She yawned while looking around the room. It was then that she noticed Maggie sitting at the island. She plopped down beside her and scratched her head.

"Since you're up early you can have breakfast with me and Emma," Johanna said.

Maggie looked at her sympathetically. "She already left, Jo."

Johanna stared at her as if she'd just spoken a foreign language. "What?"

"She already left," she repeated.

Johanna bolted from her seat and ran out of the room. If she'd not been half asleep when she came out of her room, she would've noticed that Emma wasn't sleeping on the couch. She just assumed she'd be there.

A couple of minutes later, she stumbled back into the kitchen and sat down. She stared at Maggie, unable to process what had just happened. "I can't believe she left without saying goodbye," she said.

"I know. I'm sorry."

"Why would she do that, Mags? I mean, at least she could've said goodbye."

"I know."

When the coffeemaker finished brewing a pot, Maggie made a cup for Johanna. "Here you go," she said placing the cup in front of her.

Johanna picked it up and sipped from it. She sat staring at the hot beverage while her mind was seemingly a million miles away. "What time do you think she left?" she asked glancing down at her watch.

"She probably left hours ago."

"Excuse me," Johanna said as she got up and left the kitchen. She heard Maggie call after her, but she wasn't interested in talking any longer.

She took refuge in the main level bathroom where she found herself staring at her reflection in the mirror. After a few minutes of gazing at herself in the mirror, she opened the medicine cabinet with trembling hands.

She grabbed her bottle of medicine. She was tired of taking this medicine every day, day in and day out. She was tired of having to rely on it to keep her cravings at bay. She unscrewed the top and considered pouring the rest of it down the drain. But she knew she couldn't do that. She'd come too far and whenever Emma did come back to visit, she needed to be able to welcome her with open arms.

Johanna measured out her daily dosage and took it. Today wasn't going to be the day she regressed. It would just have to wait.

After filling up and getting some snacks for the road, Emma only got in two hours of driving. She thought she'd get further by the time she had to stop, but her mind just wasn't into driving. She didn't want to be stuck in a car, driving thousands of miles back home. She wanted to be back there in Bridger, with Johanna.

By the time she made it to the first big town, she was already too fatigued to go any further. At this rate, it would probably take her an entire week to get back home to Chicago. And if it did, oh well.

All she wanted to do was sleep and since it was still early in the morning, she decided to get a room and sleep some more. She pulled into a cozy looking roadside hotel and rented a room. She didn't bother bringing any of her things with her. If she'd learned anything from her time in Bridger was that the crime rate was nearly nonexistent.

She collapsed onto the bed and groaned. She really should've said goodbye to Johanna. It made her heart ache thinking about how she must've felt when she realized that Emma was gone.

Emma had closed her eyes and was about to drift off to sleep when her phone chimed with a text message.

Johanna: Did I not deserve a goodbye?

Emma's heart clenched in her chest. She didn't even know how to respond to her question, so she left it unanswered for a couple of minutes.

Johanna: Emma?

Emma: I'm sorry.

The three little dots bounced in Johanna's message box. Emma's chest tightened with anticipation of her response. But no response came. Johanna would start typing a response but wouldn't send it. This went on for a couple of minutes.

Johanna: How far did you get?

Emma yawned and climbed under the covers. She cuddled her phone near her head and typed her response.

Emma: Not far. I guess I should've slept some more. I had to stop. I'm really tired.

Johanna: Where are you now? Are you safe?

Emma: *You are now sharing your location with Johanna*

Emma: I have no clue where I am, but I'm safe. I just sent you my location just in case I disappear.

Johanna: That's not funny.

Emma: Sorry.

Johanna: Get enough rest, okay? Sleep until your body lets you know you've had enough rest.

Emma smiled at the text. She'd just skipped out on Johanna without saying goodbye and all she was worried about was whether Emma was well rested or not.

Emma: Thanks. I'm going to go to bed now.

Johanna read the text, but she didn't reply. Emma must have waited nearly ten minutes before she realized that Johanna wasn't going to respond. Eventually sleep overtook her and she fell into a deep slumber.

Hours passed by while Emma was catching up on her rest. When her body had rested enough, sleep finally released her. She opened her eyes and was greeted with the bright early afternoon sun. She groaned and sat up in the bed. Her stomach growled like she hadn't eaten in weeks. But now that she thought about it, she realized the last thing she had eaten was around midnight.

She checked her phone expecting to have messages from Johanna but there were none from her. She only had three messages, all from Ericka inquiring about her whereabouts, her ETA, and another, again about her ETA. She rolled her eyes. It was already starting. The control and the micromanaging. That was something that she didn't miss while she was away. She decided not to answer Ericka's texts. At least not yet.

She checked the time. It was lunchtime and she could go for a buffet of some sort, but she had to settle for whatever was around. She browsed through the restaurants and services folder and found a burger joint in town that delivered and ordered her enough food to take with her on her next leg of the trip.

She tried Johanna's phone. No answer, it went straight into voicemail. Either she was working, or she was ignoring her. Emma certainly hoped it wasn't the latter. She flipped on the tv and channel surfed until she found something suitable enough to watch.

When her food came an hour later, she sat down at the table and concentrated on her meal. She wasn't even ten minutes into eating when there was a knock at the door. She checked her bags quickly.

"Delivery guy must've forgotten something," she said as she walked over to the door and opened it. Her heart nearly stopped when she realized standing on the other side was Johanna. "Oh my God. What are you doing here?"

Johanna smiled and shrugged. "I didn't get to say goodbye."

"But, how? How did you find me?" Emma said ushering her inside the room.

Johanna stepped over the threshold and quickly inspected the place. "You've been sleeping all day," she said taking out her phone. "Your location didn't move so I took a drive."

"A two-hour drive?"

"Why not?"

"Just to say goodbye?" Emma asked.

Johanna picked up a couple of fries and ate them. "Yeah, about that..." She came and stood in front of Emma, taking her gently by the shoulders. "I didn't drive this far to say goodbye to you."

"You didn't?"

"No. I came to bring you home."

"Home?"

"Yes, home. With me."

Emma's mouth dropped open. "But I can't go back just yet. I have some important things to do in Chicago."

"That's what your mouth is saying, but your heart is saying something else, isn't it?"

"What?" Emma gasped.

"Isn't it?"

Emma nodded.

"Whatever your heart is saying, listen to it. I listened to mine and that's why I'm standing here right now."

Emma sat down on the bed, her eyes stayed fixed on Johanna's as though she believed that when she blinked, Johanna would disappear. "Your heart brought you here?"

"Yes."

"Do you really want me to come back with you?"

"Would I be here if I didn't?"

"No, I guess not."

Johanna caressed Emma's face and kissed her tenderly on the forehead. "I had a lot of time to think on the trip over here and I'll tell you this one thing. Ever since you came back into my life, I've had this feeling I've never felt before. It's a feeling of finally being complete. When you left, I felt incomplete again. I hate feeling that way."

"Do you really mean that?"

"Of course, I do." She gave Emma her phone. "Look at the last picture I took in the gallery."

Emma opened the gallery and found a picture of Johanna's completed oil painting. "Wow, it's beautiful."

"That painting sat unfinished on my easel for six months. I couldn't find the inspiration to finish it because I felt like something was missing and I couldn't figure it out. Until now."

THE MISSING PIECE

Emma eyed the picture. "What was missing?"

"You were. See?" she said, pointing to the silhouette of the young woman sitting on the bench. "That's you as I saw you yesterday sitting on the bench."

Emma gasped. "It's beautiful."

"I don't have a lot to give you, but you will always have my love, Emma."

Emma choked up. "That's all I've ever really needed, you know."

"I know."

"I can't believe you want me to come back with you."

"I've lived in the past for so long I forgot what it was like to live in the present and plan for a future," she said wiping the tears from her eyes. "But if you come back home with me, we can start over fresh and start making new memories for both of us."

"Really?"

"Yes. All I want right now is to share this beautiful world with you and for you to be a part of it. Because without my daughter in my life, nothing will ever feel right."

"I want that too," Emma whispered.

Johanna hugged her tightly. "So, what do you say? Will you come back home with me?"

Emma nodded briskly. "Yes, I'd love to!"

"Great!"

Emma got up and motioned for her to join her at the table. They sat together, looking at each other and smiling. "I still can't believe you came all this way to find me," Emma said.

"Well, you drove all the way from Chicago to find me, so two hours was a piece of cake. They shared a meaningful laugh before the silence filled the air between them.

"I'm going to have to find a way to break the news to my parents," Emma said taking a bite of her burger. "But for now, they'll just have to do the galas without me."

"Thank you, Emma."

"I should be thanking you. Without you accepting me, none of this would even be possible." Emma handed a fry to Johanna and then picked one up for herself. "Here's to days ahead of learning more about each other and growing closer."

They tapped their fries together and laughed. Emma wolfed her meal down, her excitement about returning to Bridger with Johanna grew more and more. She'd been waiting for her mother her entire life, but what she didn't realize was that her mother had been waiting for her, too. As they stared at each other they realized that they'd finally found the missing piece they'd been searching for. And now their lives were complete.

THE MISSING PIECE

"Could you teach me how to ride your horse sometime?"

Johanna reached over and took her hand. "I thought you'd never ask."

www.ingramcontent.com/pod-product-compliance
Lightning Source LLC
LaVergne TN
LVHW031539060526
838200LV00056B/4574